Sapped

A Maple Syrup Mysteries Prequel

Emily James

Stronghold Books
ONTARIO, CANADA

Copyright © 2016 by Emily James.

All rights reserved. No part of this publication may be reproduced, distributed, or transmitted in any form or by any means, including photocopying, recording, or other electronic or mechanical methods, without the prior written permission of the author. It's okay to quote a small section for a review or in a school paper. To put this in plain language, this means you can't copy my work and profit from it as if it were your own. When you copy someone's work, it's stealing. No one likes a thief, so don't do it. Pirates are not nearly as cool in real life as they are in fiction.

For permission requests, write to the author at the address below.

Emily James
authoremilyjames@gmail.com
www.authoremilyjames.com

This is a work of fiction. I made it up. You are not in my book. I probably don't even know you. If you're confused about the difference between real life and fiction, you might want to call a counselor rather than a lawyer because names, characters, places, and incidents in this book are a product of my twisted imagination. Real locales and public names are sometimes used for atmospheric purposes. Any resemblance to actual people, living or dead, or to businesses, companies, events, and institutions is completely coincidental.

Book Layout ©2013 BookDesignTemplates.com
Cover Design by Deranged Doctor Designs

Sapped/ Emily James. -- 1st ed.
ISBN 978-0-9920372-7-7

To my best friend Meg, who keeps all my secrets,
even about the time when...

Make yourself an honest man, and then you may be sure there is one less rascal in the world.

–THOMAS CARLYLE

Chapter 1

I found out my boyfriend was a married man the morning I heard it on the news.

I was sliding on my second shoe and reaching for the remote control to turn off the TV before leaving for work when the red *Breaking News* text flashed across the bottom of the screen.

"Respected criminal defense attorney Peter Walsh was taken in for questioning by the police minutes ago in relation to the tragic death of his wife," the newswoman said.

I lowered my shoe to the couch and sank down beside it. The air in my apartment suddenly felt too thick to breathe. It couldn't be my Peter Walsh. Well over a million people lived and worked in Washington, DC and the surrounding counties. Surely there was more than one Peter Walsh.

But what were the odds that there was more than one Peter Walsh, criminal defense attorney?

I turned up the volume, unable to look away from the screen.

"Walsh, thirty-six, had a neighbor call 9-1-1 shortly after 6:30 this morning, claiming that his wife, thirty-two-year-old Eva Walsh, had slipped following her morning swim, hitting her head on the concrete and falling into their pool."

The image on the screen switched away from the newswoman to a shot of police leading a man from a two-story brick colonial toward a waiting police cruiser. The camera zoomed in on the man.

My Peter Walsh looked straight at the screen. Same neatly trimmed blond hair, same cleft chin, same lean frame. The rest of his appearance was the opposite of what I'd come to expect from him. His expensive suit was rumpled and wet, his tie askew, and red smeared his white shirt cuffs and down his front. Blood.

I spastically crushed the remote control. His dead wife's blood. His wife.

This couldn't be happening.

The TV switched back to the newswoman. *"We don't have much other information at this time, except that police are currently calling her death suspicious."*

My hand shook so hard that it took me three tries to turn off the TV.

I'm not sure how long I stared at the black screen. I'd been borderline late for work before the news report, but that didn't seem to matter now. My parents' law firm, where Peter and I both worked, would be in chaos after the news. It'd be a while before anyone noticed me missing.

I slumped back on the couch cushion. Everyone at the office knew he was dating me. They would either assume I'd known about his secret wife and was a willing adulteress or that I hadn't known and was therefore stupid. What kind of a woman wouldn't know that the man she'd been seeing for a *year* was married?

My skin felt all hot and clammy like I'd leaned in too close over a vegetable steamer. How could I face them? I was already the charity case of the firm, the only lawyer who'd been there longer than a year who'd never been allowed to take the lead on a case.

And now this.

An ache built in my chest, making me want to curl into a ball. I'd been publicly played. Peter came into the firm acting like a single man, which I could only assume meant he'd been looking for a mark. Maybe even hoping that by dating the bosses' daughter he could make partner in half the time. Who knew his reasons. But I had to believe that this meant every kiss and every *I love you* had been a lie.

I sucked in a few deep breaths and walled off the cascading pain. I could feel hurt over what he'd done to me later. Right now, I had to do something to salvage the situation. I couldn't bear to see disappointment on my parents' faces again or to know that my colleagues were whispering about me, taking bets on when I'd wash out as a lawyer.

Beyond that, I needed the truth from Peter—not only about whether he'd murdered his wife but about why he'd lied to me and whether I'd meant anything to him. The problem with that was, currently, no one but the police were going to be allowed anywhere near him.

The police and legal counsel.

I jammed on my missing shoe and grabbed my purse. Peter would exercise his right to a lawyer and he'd want the very best. That meant my dad.

If I could convince my dad to assign me to his case as well, I'd show people that I was capable and strong, and I'd be able to look the cheating SOB in the face and demand the truth.

My late start put me right in the middle of DC rush hour, which is the worst possible situation if you're already late, stressed, and don't want a lot of time by yourself to think.

Two exits into my drive, I glanced at the clock. I'd never make it to the office in time to catch my dad. My only hope of being part of the interview was if I headed straight to whatever police station they'd taken Peter to.

I told my phone to dial my dad.

"Edward Dawes," he answered on the first ring. He must have just ended another call because usually he was nearly impossible to reach on the phone.

I was at a disadvantage not talking to him face to face, where I could read his body language and react accordingly, so I'd have to give no corner for a refusal. "I want on Peter's case as co-counsel."

"You saw the news."

He was stalling, giving himself time to decide whether he thought I could handle this.

I bit back the urge to drum impatiently on my steering wheel. He might hear it and interpret it as a sign of weakness. "I did."

"Your mother thought you'd be a blubbering puddle. She was going to call you to tell you to take the day off."

Gee, thanks, Mom, for the vote of confidence. "I'm already on the road. You just need to tell me which station to head for."

He let out a sigh full with years of disappointment. "I don't think that's a wise idea, Nicole. This is going to be a high-profile case. His wife was a public affairs specialist for the DOD and the niece of a senator."

The first question that popped into my mind was how he already knew more about Peter's wife than I did, but asking that question would prove I couldn't maintain professional distance from this case. Especially since the answer was probably that he had our research assistants digging into her background the minute the news broke, prepping him for whatever the police might bring up during the coming interview. I was the only one racing to catch up.

"I'm not asking to be made the lead. It'd be the wrong time for that." Given my track record with speaking in front of groups, any time would likely be the wrong time for that. "I'm only asking to be a part of it. You know I'm the best person you have when it comes to talking to witnesses one on one."

I had him there. I might be awkward as a thirteen-year-old talking to her secret crush when I was in the courtroom, but when it came to personal interactions, I had a knack for reading people and getting them to open up to me.

Horns blaring in the background filled his pause and meant he was already on the road, too. I could almost see him weighing the pros and cons in his head.

"Call the office and get the address." His voice was all business again. "But you're not getting special treatment because you're my daughter. First strike and you're off the case."

Chapter 2

Apparently my recently widowed ex-boyfriend lived in Fairfax—yet another fact I hadn't known about him before this morning. Peter always cited the commute when I suggested we go to his place instead of mine. And it'd seemed like a legit reason at the time. No one in this area added extra time to their commute if they could help it.

In hindsight, that "Let's go to your place, not mine" line probably should have been a red flag.

I parked next to my dad's black Audi in front of the stately brown stone Fairfax City Police Department building. The humid August air flattened my hair and plastered my clothes to my body. Which was perfect. My dad would immediately notice that I looked wilted.

I swear the man wasn't human. He managed to look freshly starched even when the air was thick enough to swim through.

Off to the right, three girls squealed and chased each other around the playground equipment on the edge of Van Dyke Park. It made me smile despite the situation. One of the things I loved about the DC area was the way the city wound in among the greenery, almost like it was ancient ruins being reclaimed by nature. It wasn't like some urban spaces where all you saw were sharp edges, metal, and concrete.

My dad hovered inside the front doors, and based on the way he flicked his wrist to glance at his watch, he'd been there for at least five minutes. His gaze ran over my appearance, and he pursed his lips but said nothing about it. He didn't have to.

I smoothed my hair and fluffed my clothing as discreetly as I could.

He ushered me down the hallway. "I've already seen Peter and advised him, but he's insisting he wants to answer their questions. Given the circumstances, that's probably for the best. Refusing would make him look guilty."

That wasn't always the advice my dad gave to clients. Guilt or innocence aside, it depended on the situation and how many viable interpretations there were of it.

It's about controlling perception, he'd once told me. *The objective truth matters less than people's subjective perception of it.*

Goosebumps raised on my arms, and I shivered. Must be the sudden switch to the air conditioning after the heat outside.

Captain Timothy Rochon waited at the end of the hallway. I recognized him from the media. His stance telegraphed impatience. He caught my dad's gaze, inclined his head toward a door, and went inside.

My dad blocked my progress with his arm and angled to face me, his back to the room Captain Rochon disappeared into.

"You're to observe only." He gripped my wrist. "You're not to talk in there. Do you understand me?"

Something flickered in his eyes—nervousness? The cold around me crawled into my core. I gave a sharp nod and he let me go.

We filed into the seats waiting for us on the same side of the table as Peter. Another officer already sat next to Captain Rochon.

Peter pulled his chair closer to the table, and the chair legs scraped across the floor. He wore a dark gray jumpsuit that the police must have given him after taking his clothes for evidence. His hair was still damp, and the odor of chlorine clogged the air.

He didn't meet my gaze, but that was for the best. Now wasn't an ideal time to announce to the police that he'd been having an affair, and my hands twitched with the urge to toss his glass of water into his face.

I tuned out the back and forth posturing between Rochon and my dad. Maybe I should have been studying my dad and how he managed to balance showing respect with maintaining the upper hand, but my insides felt hollow. Coming here might not have been such a good idea after all, and it was too late to back out now.

Rochon asking Peter to walk them through what happened this morning snapped my focus back where it belonged.

"I was upstairs getting ready for work. I heard Eva's cell ringing downstairs—I remember because it was her ringtone, so I didn't go down to get it the way I would if it was mine—and then I heard a scream."

His hands rested on the edge of the table, his body language open. Normally I would have read it as a sign of honesty, but not anymore. Not with Peter, at least. Clearly I couldn't read him at all because he would have had to lie to me multiple times in the past year to keep his wife a secret, and I hadn't caught any of his lies. I clenched my own hands in my lap.

"What time was that?" Rochon asked.

Peter shrugged. "I didn't take the time to look at a clock, but I'd guess quarter after six or so. Like I said, I was getting ready for work."

His shrug seemed almost too casual, but again, I didn't know how much of the situation I was reading through my anger. Did I want him to be guilty of killing his wife? The idea of him being punished held a certain appeal after how he'd treated both her and me by cheating.

Guilt twisted my stomach. If he was innocent, I couldn't wish prison on him, not even as recompense for deceiving me.

Rochon gave a keep-going nod. "So you heard a scream and then what?"

"I ran downstairs and out onto the pool deck. That's when I saw Eva." His voice cracked, and he ran his hands through his hair. "I saw Eva in the pool. The water was red all around her. I thought she must have been running for the phone and slipped."

My heart twisted, sending pain through my chest. I bit the inside of my cheek to keep from showing any emotion. He sounded like he loved her.

He sounded like he loved you, too, a tiny voice whispered in the back of my head.

That was true. I didn't know what to believe anymore. Could he have loved us both?

Peter drew in a shuddering breath. "I pulled her from the pool. She wasn't breathing so I started CPR. I think our neighbor, Hong Li, must have heard Eva scream as well because the next thing I knew she was calling over the fence, asking if we were alright. I told her to call 9-1-1."

My dad was staying exceptionally quiet. I guess he'd already gone over this with Peter before I arrived.

"We'll be checking into all that," Rochon said.

He glanced up at the nearly imperceptible camera set high on the wall. His chin dipped slightly. Direction to whoever was on the other side to check something? It was noticing small ticks like that which kept me my job. The police thought there was a hole in Peter's story.

"We have talked to two of your neighbors already," Rochon continued. "One reported hearing you and your wife yelling at each other a couple nights ago. What were you fighting about?"

Peter gave that too-practiced shrug again. "I don't remember."

"You don't remember?"

"Captain." My dad rapped his pen sharply on the table. "Do you remember every argument you've had with your wife? Married people argue. It doesn't mean anything."

"It means quite a bit when one of those people ends up dead two days later."

My heart felt like I'd drunk one too many Red Bulls. The fact that my previously silent father cut off the questioning on that point meant a lot actually. It meant he either knew or guessed that whatever they'd been fighting about would make Peter look guilty.

My dad slid his pen back into his shirt pocket. "We're here as a courtesy because my client loved his wife and wants to resolve any questions as quickly as possible so the family can grieve in peace. If you're going to turn this into a witch hunt, we're leaving."

Rochon rose to his feet. "We want to give those who loved her"—his gaze slid to Peter in a way that hinted he didn't think Peter fell into that category—"closure as much as you do. We appreciate Mr. Walsh's patience, and if he could wait here a little longer while we try to sort out a few remaining details, it would be a great help in resolving this unfortunate tragedy smoothly."

Point scored for Rochon. Now Peter couldn't walk out, not if he wanted to maintain the appearance of a grief-stricken husband. They wanted to keep him for some reason.

Rochon motioned to the officer with him, and they both left the room.

I leaned in close to my dad. "They're waiting on something they think will let them charge him."

"Any idea what?"

I shook my head. "Rochon gave very little away, but they're checking on some detail behind the scenes. I couldn't get anything more. He's a hard read."

But so was Peter. If Rochon picked up on some part of his story as potentially untrue, I didn't know what part.

"I'll go see what I can find out," my dad said.

He left the room, and then it was just Peter and me. Alone.

He drew in a loud breath, breaking the silence first. "Thank you for coming. I know you wouldn't be here unless you'd volunteered to be."

I'd had so many things I wanted to ask him and wanted to say, but they all log-jammed together in my throat. Only one really mattered.

Since we had no expectation of privacy in a police station, I moved closer and kept my voice low. "Did you kill her?"

It was the one question we were never supposed to ask a client, especially while sitting in a police station. But he wasn't a client to me. He was my boyfriend—ex-boyfriend—who very well might be arrested for his wife's murder within the hour.

Peter sat back a fraction and opened his mouth, then snapped it shut. It was a first. I'd caught him off guard. "You know me better than that."

Whether it was a dodge or genuine hurt feelings, it wasn't going to work on me. "I thought I did. I also thought you were single."

"Fair enough." He rubbed the side of his nose. "No, I didn't kill her. We weren't in love anymore, but we were still friends. I never would have hurt her." He glanced at the door as if he expected Captain Rochon to return any minute. "And I never meant to hurt you." His voice had dropped to a whisper.

I wrapped my arms around myself. Intent only mattered when it came to murder. In every other case, the result meant everything.

He tilted his upper body forward and stretched a hand partway across the space between us. “You’re the only one I can count on to believe me. I assumed what happened to Eva was an accident, but if the police find out that it’s not, it means someone out there killed my wife, and I’m going to be blamed for her death.

Chapter 3

A prickling sensation ran over my skin, and the hair on my arms stood up. This was the first suggestion I'd heard that someone else might be involved. The question I needed to answer was whether this was Peter reaching or whether this was a real possibility.

Peter's hand continued to stretch toward me, but he didn't make contact. "A few days ago, I thought I saw a former client sitting in a car outside my house. A client whose trial I screwed up. If he wanted—"

The door swung open, cutting off Peter's theory and my chance to ask him any questions.

Captain Rochon and the other officer entered first, followed by my dad.

It took all my self-control not to suck in a loud breath. The lines around my dad's mouth seemed harder and his wrinkles a bit deeper. I knew that look. It was the *things aren't going my way* look. The look that meant someone, somewhere, was going to have hell to pay.

Thank whatever higher power might exist that it wasn't directed at me this time.

Compared to my dad, Rochon practically had canary feathers hanging from his jaws. He laid a brown folder down on the table. "Thank you for your patience, Peter."

It was *Peter* now rather than *Mr. Walsh*. That was an extremely bad sign.

Rochon tapped his fingers on the folder. "We need to clarify a couple more things with you, and then we'll get you out of this room."

I traced the wood grain in the table with a fingernail. Perhaps I was reading too much into Rochon's choice of words, but I couldn't help but notice that he said *out of this room* rather than *out of here*.

If Peter or my dad noticed as well, neither of them let on.

"You said you heard your wife scream, and you ran downstairs to check on her," Rochon said. "You assume she slipped and hit her head because you found her in the water, bleeding. Is that correct?"

"That's correct." Peter's voice sounded the same way a person treading a balance beam looked.

Rochon opened the folder and slid a photo across the table toward Peter. The picture seemed innocent enough at first glance—a close-up of stamped concrete next to an in-ground pool.

On second glance, a rusty red splotch that could only be blood stood out.

My mouth went dry. The distance between the blood stain and the pool could be deceiving in the picture, but I was pretty sure I knew where Rochon was going with this.

Rochon drew an imaginary line on the photo from the blood stain to the pool. "How far do you think that is?"

"What does this have to do with anything?" my dad asked.

Rochon kept his gaze focused on Peter. A muscle spasmed at the corner of Peter's eye—the first sign of stress I'd seen him show. Peter shook his head.

"We measured." Rochon pulled the photo back toward him. "It's five feet. If your wife fell here," he pressed a finger into the blood stain, "then how did she fall all the way over here into the pool?"

He hopped his finger over to the pool.

Peter raised his gaze from the image and looked Rochon in the eyes. "I don't know. I found her in the pool. I didn't see her fall in."

My dad folded his hands on top of the table and leaned back in his chair. "Alright, Peter. That's enough. I think we've reached the point in this interview where you don't need to say any more. These questions aren't looking to find out how Eva *accidentally* died anymore."

No, they weren't. We were going through the motions as they laid out their case before arresting him. I peeked at my dad. His granite expression said he'd known it when he came back into the room.

Instead of controlling impressions, this now became about damage control. My dad would let this play out because he had to, but he wouldn't let Peter speak again.

Rochon shoved the next picture toward Peter.

The damage to the back of Eva's skull.

My stomach rolled, and I looked away, focusing on the black scuff mark on the wall across from me. This was another part I'd never been good at. The photos of the deceased. The combination of the gore and the lost life. It always hit me in the heart and the stomach at the same time.

My dad flipped the photo face down. "My client saw enough of his wife's injuries earlier when he was trying to save her life. He doesn't need to be reminded."

Rochon flipped the picture back over and nudged it even closer. "I thought your client might like a chance to explain how a woman who fell accidentally had two wounds on her head. Close together, like someone bashed her skull into the concrete, realized she was still conscious, and did it again."

My dad rose to his feet and put a hand on Peter's shoulder. "Get up, Peter. They're either going to charge you or we're leaving."

Rochon got to his feet as well. "Peter Walsh, you're under arrest for the murder of your wife."

They gave Peter one more chance to confess and take a plea deal. He rejected it, ignoring my dad's signal that they should discuss it.

As they were leading Peter out, he turned to look back over his shoulder. *Help me*, he mouthed.

I sank back down into a chair in the empty room and massaged my temples. The tension pooled there wouldn't release. He'd lied to me about being married, albeit a lie of omission. But that didn't necessarily make him a murderer.

The pleading look on his face as they took him away played across my mind again. It hurt something in my heart.

I had to prove him innocent. For his sake and mine. Because if I'd been played a second time, I wasn't sure I'd be able to trust anyone again.

When my dad and I finally left the police station, the air had the ozone smell of an impending storm.

I trailed him around to the driver's side of his car. Peter's arrest would be on every six o'clock newscast in the DC area. We couldn't protect him from being tried and convicted in the media before he was even assigned a court date, but we could start preparing to make sure he wouldn't be convicted when his case actually came before a judge.

"So what are our next steps? We need to prove he didn't do this. He mentioned an old client hanging around his house recently. I thought maybe we should start there."

My dad's shoulders had an unusual slump to them, and for a moment, he looked his full sixty years. Normally, his energy and bearing made his actual age impossible to guess.

I was being selfish. I'd only thought about myself. I hadn't thought about how this must have hit my dad. As far as I knew, he'd never had to defend one of his own before. And Peter was his rising star.

I rubbed a hand along his upper arm. "I'm sorry, Daddy."

He brushed his fingers across the top of my shoulder, so quick I might have imagined it. I knew I hadn't though. That quick finger brush was as close as we'd come to hugging since I was five or six.

He touched his key fob and his car beeped. "You need to remember that proving Peter innocent isn't our job. Our job is to get him acquitted."

I kept my mouth closed by force of will alone. Guilt or innocence didn't matter in my parents' world. All that mattered was the jury's verdict. But this wasn't any other client. This was Peter. Their employee. My boyfriend...ex-boyfriend. This was someone we knew and cared about. Surely proving him innocent mattered this time.

"This will follow him everywhere unless we prove he didn't do it." I planted myself firmly at the edge of his door so that he couldn't open it unless I moved. My dad had a habit of ending conversations by leaving when he felt they were over. This time, the conversation was going to end when I said so. "If his reputation doesn't matter to you, then surely the reputation of your firm by association matters."

My dad glanced at his door handle. I leaned my hip into it.

His eyes hardened. "Peter's not returning to the firm no matter how this turns out. We won't make the announcement until after the jury renders their verdict, but he's done at Fitzhenry & Dawes."

The air rushed from my lungs, and I straightened. "Even though he didn't do it?"

My dad gave me his stone-faced look, the same one he gave to law enforcement officers who asked questions he felt they should have been smart enough not to try.

He wasn't an unfair man. The reason he'd become a criminal attorney in the first place was that he believed in *innocent until proven guilty* and that everyone deserved a chance to mount a defense. So if firing Peter wasn't about his current arrest, then it could only be about one thing. "Is this because he lied about being married?"

"That's part of it, yes."

Warmth curled around my heart. With him being my boss, and with my skills as a lawyer being the exact opposite of Babe Ruth's skills in baseball, it was easy to forget he was also my dad. Where he failed in showing affection, he excelled at standing as a shield between me and anything that tried to harm me.

He took my elbow and moved me out of his way before I gathered my thoughts enough to resist. He slid inside the car and closed the door, but rolled down his window. "I don't want to hear anything more about proving Peter innocent. You shouldn't be on this case at all, and you know it."

I cringed inwardly. He was right about that. Technically, my involvement was a conflict of interest since I could just as easily be considered a suspect in Peter's wife's murder. I could see the headline now *Criminal Attorney's Wife Murdered by His Secret Mistress.*

My dad started the car, and the engine purred softly to life. "If you want to stay on this case, you're going to do exactly what I tell you and stay out of the spotlight. Since there's nothing else we can do today, I want you to take the rest of the day off and get your head on straight."

Get my head on straight? Like I didn't have enough self-control to handle this?

"You looked close to losing it a couple times during the interview today," he said. "You do that too often and the police are going to wonder why."

It was like he read my thoughts. He did have a point. "But you're going to let me stay on the case?"

I needed to stay on the case. Without access, I wouldn't be able to prove that Peter didn't do this. And regardless of what my dad thought, that did matter.

"For now. Once the evidence comes in, I'll need you to review it. No one else has your eye for detail."

Before I could even feel the warm glow again from his compliment, his window zipped back up and he backed his car away.

I pulled my cell phone from my purse and dialed Ahanti's number. I wanted her to hear about this from me rather than see it on the news. I'm pretty sure that was part of the best friend contract.

Besides, since I had the rest of the day off, I needed someone to join me as I ate my way through a tub of chocolate fudge ice cream. Stress eating was like drinking—you should never do it alone.

Chapter 4

When the district attorney finally sent over copies of the evidence they had against Peter, the file was small. They had enough to arrest him, but they'd continue to build their case over the coming months.

As promised, I'd been tasked to go through it to try to work out a preliminary list of holes and alternative explanations. My dad wanted them for Peter's trial. I planned to use them to figure out who actually killed Eva Walsh.

I set up my phone to record and upload my dictated notes to the shared Cloud folder on the case. It was a new system my dad wanted us to try. The theory behind it was that it would make information sharing between members working a case easier and prevent duplicated work. Each portion of the evidence that I catalogued would be saved as a separately named audio file, and a secretary would transcribe it later, indexing it as well.

It seemed like extra steps and busy work to me, but I wasn't the boss.

I flipped open the first folder. It held the autopsy photos and report. I skipped the photos, but checked the report. As we'd already found out from the police, Eva Walsh had two wounds to her head, close enough together that the most likely explanation was someone had bashed her head into the cement. I briefly noted that information.

"Second file." My voice sounded strange in the emptiness of my office. It felt a bit crazy talking to myself. "Crime scene photos."

I skimmed the investigator's notes first this time before looking at the photos.

"No signs of any forced entry into their home, and no evidence or witnesses of anyone jumping their privacy fence."

That didn't look good for Peter. One of the things we'd need to do is show how the real killer could have entered their backyard and have done so without Eva noticing them. Maybe she knew them and let them in? That would only be a viable idea if the former client Peter saw hanging around his house wasn't involved. Eva Walsh surely wouldn't have let him in.

I didn't dictate those thoughts into my notes. My dad wouldn't approve. He only wanted *the pertinent facts*, as he put it, not my hopeful speculation.

"Cell phone records show Eva Walsh did receive a call at 6:22 am. Duration five seconds, suggesting the call went to voicemail, but the caller didn't leave a message. Phone number belonged to an unregistered disposable cell."

I slid the call records to the side. The next pictures in the file were of Eva's cell phone. It had a silver and black bejeweled cover, flashy like I'd have expected from someone who worked regularly with the press but not so flashy that it looked unprofessional for someone working on a contract for the government. The case had a vertical crack that ran almost the entire length of the phone, and a tiny piece had chipped away.

"Crime scene investigators found her phone on the kitchen counter, inside the door leading to the pool deck."

That part at least confirmed Peter's story that he heard her phone ringing downstairs moments before he heard her scream. What it didn't explain was why Eva's killer would have taken that moment to attack her. Maybe she was distracted by the ringing phone. Or maybe they seized the opportunity to try to make it look like a slip-and-fall accident, but that seemed like it left a lot to chance. Unless they'd planned it all along and had made the call themselves.

The files didn't hold anything else worth recording except a few notes about the Walshes' finances. Both had a substantial life insurance policy that listed the other as the primary beneficiary. Their bank records didn't show any signs of financial trouble. Eva was apparently a trust fund baby who didn't actually need to work.

I worried my bottom lip between my teeth. As much as I wanted to dislike her, the fact that she chose to work even though she could have spent her days going to the spa and shopping deserved respect.

I clicked off my phone's recorder, scanned the sheet that listed the witnesses, and uploaded it as well. As we interviewed each witness, the person who interviewed them would add a link from the witness list to their notes. The witness list was a short list at this point. John and Alice Reed heard an argument between Peter and Eva two nights before her death, but couldn't make out what was being said. Hong Li, the neighbor on the left, heard Eva's scream and was the one who called 9-1-1 for help, just as Peter said.

I swept all the physical files together and attached a sticky note to the front, letting anyone who came for them know I'd already dictated them into the online shared folder.

The police's evidence so far hadn't given me much to go on. The best way to get a sense of how someone might have pulled off this murder would be to walk the crime scene.

Expectation is a powerful force. The police had assumed Peter killed Eva, so they might have overlooked evidence that could point to another suspect. I would be going in with the opposite belief.

Peter had left a set of keys with my dad while he was waiting to make bail. Getting in would be easy. The only question was whether I could handle going to the house Peter shared with his wife. The thought alone made me feel like I was coming down with the flu.

But if I didn't want to go alone, who could I safely bring? I certainly didn't want to bring anyone from work. Talk about awkward.

Since the police had already released the crime scene, I didn't necessarily have to bring anyone official. I dug out my phone and dialed Ahanti.

Ahanti met me out front of Peter's house in her bright purple Smart Car. It looked like someone tossed it in a giant trash compactor, with only two seats and nothing behind. But every time someone mocked it, Ahanti asked them how much they spent on gas each month. Then she was the one mocking them.

The curtains next door swished to the side and fell back into place. It'd happened when I climbed out of my car as well. If the neighbor wanted something to gossip about, he or she was going to get it as soon as they saw Ahanti.

She folded herself out of her tiny car, long legs first followed by her Roaring Twenties-style dress. Tattoos she'd designed herself colored the bronze skin of her bare arms and shoulders, and today she'd pulled her red-streaked black hair up into a casual ponytail. Not the kind of person I expected the neighbors normally saw around here.

Not the kind of person my parents would have picked for my best friend, either, but Ahanti and I had been like sisters since the day she moved into the apartment next to mine and the Chinese delivery man tried to deliver her order to my apartment.

"You're a better soul than I am," Ahanti said as she came up Peter's front steps. "I was hatching plans for how to sneak into his cell and tattoo his face in the night."

Ahanti was one of the most in-demand tattoo artists in the DC area. She didn't take walk-ins at her shop. If someone wanted her to work on their tattoos, they needed to book a slot up to six months in advance. If given the chance, she could have made Peter look like the Joker from Batman or she could have stenciled on Hannibal Lector's mask. Or maybe just branded CHEATER across his forehead.

"You should have told me sooner. I would have liked to see what you came up with for him." I'd meant it to come out light, but I ended up sounding sad. "We'd better go inside before the neighbor calls the police."

I jutted my chin toward the once-again-fluttering window curtain.

Ahanti followed me into the house. "What are we looking for?"

That was the trick. I didn't know. I hoped I'd know it when I saw it. "Anything that could give us an idea of what really happened here or who might have wanted Eva Walsh dead."

I stopped in their entryway, and my breath seemed to thicken in my lungs. Peter had lived with his wife in my dream house. A curved staircase with a mahogany banister wove its way upstairs to the right, and the rest of the downstairs was open concept, giving me a view of the fireplace and two-story ceiling in the living room, straight through to the chef's kitchen with the glass door that led outside. Granted, I didn't usually have time to cook, so I don't know what good a chef's kitchen would have done me, but the idea of experimenting in the kitchen appealed to some artistic spark buried deep inside. Probably the same subjugated spark that connected with Ahanti.

"You okay?" Ahanti asked softly.

"I will be." I set up the voice recording program on my phone and linked it to the Cloud again, but kept it paused until we located something worth recording. "Let's divide up the area."

Ahanti headed for the hall closet, and I bypassed the living room, where the only thing of interest seemed to be smiling pictures of Peter and Eva. I didn't need to see those. I stopped next to the spot on the counter where Eva's phone had been.

From where I stood, I had a clear view out across the pool. A small oval table lay on its side between two chairs on the pool deck, probably knocked over by the emergency responders in their attempts to save Eva.

I slid open the glass door and headed outside, closing the door behind me to keep from air conditioning the outdoors. A seven-foot-high privacy fence wrapped around the entirety of the yard. I snapped a picture of the yard and the overturned table to upload just in case.

Something in the edge of the grass glinted in the sun.

I knelt down. A tiny triangle-shaped silver-and-black sliver wedged in the grass at the edge of the pool deck. It looked like it might have come off Eva Walsh's cell phone cover. I snapped a zoomed-in photo to be safe, but it wasn't likely it mattered to the case. Eva's phone was inside at the time of her death, and her cell phone cover could have broken any time prior.

The glass door rattled behind me, and I shot to my feet, my heart beating at the bottom of my throat.

"Jumpy much?" Ahanti said from the now-open door. "Didn't you hear me? I was calling you."

"Sorry." I brushed off the knees of my pants. "You know how I laser focus."

"Yeah, don't do that when you're out in the world, okay? With the way you sometimes zone out when you're thinking, you could walk out in the middle of traffic and not know it." She grabbed my hand. "Now come see what I found. I don't know if it's important, but I think Peter's wife might have been packing."

Packing could be significant in a couple of ways. If they were both packing, it could signal financial troubles the police hadn't found yet. If it was only Eva packing, it could mean she'd found out about Peter's affair—which wouldn't look good for Peter—or it could mean she was having an affair as well and planning to leave him for her lover. That could give us another potential suspect for her murder.

Ahanti led the way up the stairs. She shot an apologetic look back over her shoulder. "The box I found is in the master bedroom."

Ugg. Their bedroom most definitely ranked at the top of my list of places I *didn't* want to go right now.

I straightened my shoulders. I could do this. Be a professional, Nicole. Be a professional.

I kept my gaze averted from their bed—I didn't need any mental images popping into my head—and beelined for the box. It was only a single box. That didn't say *packing* to me.

I shifted it out away from the wall. On the back side, written in big block letters were the words FOR GOODWILL. "Looks like it's a box of old stuff she was giving away."

"Guess I'm not the best detective." Ahanti frowned and pulled a pale pink blouse from the box. "But in my defense, most of these look like they've only been worn once. Who donates new clothes?"

I peeked inside the walk-in closet next to the box. Every hanger was full, and many of the outfits still had tags on them. So my assessment of Eva Walsh earlier wasn't exact. She did seem to spend quite a bit of time shopping, but at least she donated what she no longer wanted.

I held back a sigh. Once again, it was hard to fault her. From what little I'd seen of her so far, it was difficult to understand why Peter cheated on her. Especially with someone like me.

"Should I have realized he was married?"

Ahanti stuffed the skirt she'd been examining back into the box and flopped the lid shut. "Some men are really good liars. No one at work knew he was married either, right?"

I nodded.

"Then I wouldn't stress over it."

"But they weren't dating him."

She turned me around back toward the door and directed me down the stairs. "What else do we still need to see while we're here?"

There wasn't really anything. In fact, if I was being honest with myself, I probably hadn't needed to come at all. At least not for the case. I think I had needed to come for me. To see the other side of the double life he'd been leading. I wasn't someone who was easily deceived, and yet he'd managed it. He'd not only lied to me, but he'd made me doubt the one skill that made me feel confident and competent and worthwhile.

And despite all that, I was still fighting to clear his name, like I had some warped version of Stockholm syndrome. "Do you think I'm pathetic for wanting to prove he didn't kill his wife?"

"I'd think you were pathetic if you kept dating him, but not for trying to get him off the murder charge." She shrugged. "Parts of your relationship weren't real, but that doesn't mean they didn't feel real to you."

Heaviness settled in my chest. It had felt real. Peter was my first long-term relationship. The last few weeks, I'd started to want him to also be my last.

I didn't know how to move on from that. How did I keep this from coloring every relationship I'd have in the future?

Assuming I had any, of course. All my previous relationship attempts had aborted as soon as we got past the polite getting-to-know-you stage and they realized that I wasn't the kind of woman who'd help make us a power couple. Usually when I laughed so hard I snorted, accidentally knocked over their glass of red wine onto their $3000 suit, or revealed my secret geek streak by forgetting to put away my complete collection of *Star Wars* DVDs before inviting them over. The men who might have actually liked who I was never even asked me out, scared away by my last name and career.

"Nicole?" Ahanti waved a hand in front of my face. "You still in there somewhere?"

The temperature in the room seemed to have increased by five degrees. "Sorry. Again. I guess I'm still processing."

Ahanti cocked her head to the side. "You know what would make you feel better?"

"What?"

"If you let me give you a tattoo. I'd make sure you could hide it under your clothes. Promise."

I shuddered. "Thanks but no thanks. Unless you can come up with a needle-free tattooing method, I'm still going to pass."

"I'm going to convince you one day." She swept a hand in an arc that encompassed the room. "We done here? I'm starving. We can get Chinese to cheer you up, and I'll even let you have my fortune cookie."

"Almost done." I should come back at some point and talk to the watchful neighbor, but that could wait. For right now, something about the backyard niggled at my mind. I couldn't bring it into focus. "I want to take one more look outside."

We went back out and stood side by side on the pool deck.

"Okay, Monk," Ahanti said. "What are we looking for?"

I'd recently hooked her on the old USA Network show with the obsessive-compulsive detective. She still tried to pretend she was only watching it for my sake, but she kept returning one season's DVD and asking for the next one more frequently than someone who was slogging through a show for the sake of their friend would have.

"I'm not actually Monk-like, am I?"

"Nah, but I don't know any other detectives to compare you to." She tightened the tie on her ponytail and shielded her eyes. "So...what are we looking for this time?"

I walked around the pool once. Nothing looked abnormal.

I stepped around the overturned table on my way back to Ahanti. My fingers itched at the sight of it lying there. Since I'd already taken a picture and the police had cleared the scene, what harm could there be? I hoisted it upright. Maybe I was a little like Monk after all. "If you had a table out here beside the pool, would you leave your phone inside on the kitchen counter?"

"Maybe. If I didn't want to get it wet when I got out of the pool." Her gaze shifted downward, toward her feet and the rust-colored splotch on the deck. "Is that blood?"

Her face took on an honest-to-goodness green tint.

I pressed a hand over my mouth to smother a laugh. "You see blood when you work, don't you?"

She backed a step away. "That's different."

"Uh huh." Since I'd put the table back, I shifted the off-kilter planter back into place, too, and brushed some spilled dirt off the edge of the deck. "I think this was a dead end. I'll have to start talking to—"

My phone rang in my pocket. I fished it out, ended the paused upload, and answered.

"Nicole Fitzhenry-Dawes."

"This is Captain Rochon with the Fairfax City Police Department. I believe we met the other day when you sat in as co-counsel for Peter Walsh."

A hard ball formed in the pit of my stomach. There was no good reason Rochon would call me rather than my dad about the case. "I was."

"Could you come down to the station? I have a few questions I'd like to ask you."

Chapter 5

The amount I was sweating this time when I entered the Fairfax City Police Department had nothing to do with the heat. If I was right about why they'd called me down here, my parents were going to lecture me for an hour when they found out I hadn't called them. But arriving with a lawyer in tow seemed like a great way to shout *I have a guilty conscience* to the police.

I didn't have a guilty conscience. Whoever killed Eva Walsh, I could at least be certain it wasn't me.

Captain Rochon greeted me in the foyer. "Thank you for coming down, Ms. Fitzhenry-Dawes."

I didn't realize it was optional, I felt like saying. But I didn't say it. Because antagonizing the police is never a good idea.

"I'm happy to help, but I'm a bit confused about why I'm here." Playing naïve, however, was usually a great way to see if you could weasel a bit of information out of someone else that they wouldn't otherwise have given. "My father's the lead on Mr. Walsh's case, so communication should really go through him."

Rochon opened the door to a much smaller room than the one we'd been in the day they arrested Peter. "I think we both realize I haven't asked you here as Peter Walsh's legal representation."

He closed the door with an ominous click. Ominous to me, at least. I might have made a huge mistake coming alone. There was only one reason I could possibly be here—they'd found out about the affair and they wanted to use it against Peter.

Rochon took a chair on the same side of the table as me rather than across. He slung an arm across the back on his chair and angled toward me.

If I had Spidey-sense, it would have been tingling. Every choice he'd made about positioning and posture since we'd entered this room was carefully selected. He was going to invade my personal space to put pressure on me while at the same time trying to come across as someone who wanted to help me.

He quickly read me my rights, claiming it was standard procedure, as if I wouldn't know better. The purpose of the interview suddenly tilted toward using whatever I said against me as well as against Peter. Did they think we'd conspired together to kill his wife?

"May I call you Nicole?" Rochon smiled, but his lips stayed flat across the top, making it look stiff and awkward. "*Fitzhenry-Dawes* is a bit of a mouthful."

"Nicole is fine." I made a show of checking my watch. *Even if you're panicking inside, never let them see it,* my mom always said about sitting in when the police interviewed a client. It probably applied even more when the police were interviewing you. "Now why did you call me down here? I have dinner plans with a friend in half an hour."

"Some interesting information came up today during interviews with Peter's coworkers."

And now I had a choice to make. Did I wait for him to come out with what he'd discovered, or did I simply stop the parrying we'd been doing and admit to dating Peter? Both my parents would say not to give them anything unless I was positive how they were going to use it, but Rochon was a trained investigator. Continuing with the act likely wouldn't do anything but waste both our time and make me look guilty.

"So I'm here because they told you Peter and I were dating."

I didn't make it a question. It wasn't, and we both knew it.

Rochon leaned a little closer. "You weren't exactly forthcoming with that information."

His voice had taken on that half-chastising, half-amused tone, like I was a child who'd done something exceptionally naughty that was also exceptionally funny. It said *we'll overlook that little gaffe if you tell me the truth now.*

A muscle twitched in my cheek, and I clenched my teeth together before I could stop myself. He saw me as the weak link. The one whose confidence he might be able to gain. The one he might be able to trick into saying something they could use.

Even though it probably shouldn't have, it hurt more than all my parents' and coworkers' lack of confidence in me. Rochon didn't know me. I might not be the best lawyer, but I was no weak link. Just because I couldn't speak eloquently in public and I was a little klutzy didn't mean I was stupid. But that's how he saw me.

I leaned back and crossed my arms over my chest. "It wasn't relevant."

"Your boyfriend's accused of murdering his wife, and you don't think his affair with you was relevant?"

"Ex-boyfriend. And it would only be relevant if he did murder his wife, but I don't believe he did."

"Ex-boyfriend."

Crap, crap, and double crap. *Way to go, Nicole.* I'd made myself sound bitter and quite possibly like someone who would have killed Eva Walsh and framed Peter. I'd let my wounded pride cloud my better judgment.

I wanted to drop my head into my hands and massage my temples, but I couldn't.

I should have called one of my parents to come here with me.

"When did your relationship with Peter Walsh end?" Rochon asked in a too-casual tone.

I had the right to remain silent, but this seemed like the worst possible moment to choose to exercise that right if I didn't want to end up charged with Eva Walsh's murder in Peter's place or right alongside him as a co-conspirator. Was this desperate desire to sort themselves out of a mess what our clients felt while my dad was telling them not to say anything more? He'd probably be saying that to me right now, but I hadn't done anything wrong and I didn't want to look like I had because I refused to answer a simple question.

"When I found out from the news that he was a brand-new widower."

"You didn't know he was married while you were dating?"

"I did not."

Rochon sat up straighter and the casualness dropped from him like a towel. "Because it's starting to look a little like you might have found out and killed Eva Walsh so that you could have Peter to yourself. Or perhaps you two planned this together."

"That doesn't make sense. If I'd killed his wife so that I could be with him, why would he be my *ex*-boyfriend now?"

Rochon's eyes narrowed. Aaannnd I'd managed to make the situation even worse. I should have let him continue to underestimate me, and I should have asked for a lawyer. I'd played this all wrong. This was exactly why I shouldn't be practicing law. And exactly why lawyers shouldn't represent themselves.

"Breaking off the relationship in the short term would be a great way to divert suspicion," Rochon said. "If you'd like to tell us the truth in exchange for a more lenient sentence, now would be the time."

"I've told you the truth." I'm sure he'd heard that a million times from people who'd told so many lies *they'd* even lost track of the truth. It was long past time to end this. I wasn't going to continue in my foolishness. I rose to my feet. "Are you going to charge me with something? Because if you're not, you'll have to excuse me. I have a dinner date."

Rochon stood as well and opened the door for me. "We'll be in touch, Ms. Fitzhenry-Dawes."

I held my shoulders in the perfect posture my mother had drilled into me since I took my first steps and strode from the station as if his words didn't worry me at all. As soon as I slid into my car, shaking started in my legs and traveled up until my whole body shook like I was riding a bus on a potholed road.

I leaned my head back against the headrest and dialed my dad's cell phone number.

"Edward Dawes."

"Daddy." My throat closed, making the words an effort. "I think I screwed up."

Chapter 6

My father cursed, and I shrank back into his oversized home office chair.

"I know now that I should have called you or Mom right away." I tucked my feet up next to me like I was a little kid again. I'd expected him to be upset, but I hadn't expected this level of anger. My father was old school. He never swore in front of a woman and certainly never in front of me. "But wouldn't bringing a lawyer along with me have made me look suspicious, too?"

He clumped a glass down on his desk and poured himself a finger's depth of Scotch from his end-of-the-workday bottle. "Why would that have been suspicious? We could have claimed that we thought the interview was about new evidence regarding Peter's case. You have to learn to think, Nicole, before you act."

I slumped slightly. I hadn't thought about that. It wouldn't have made me look guilty to have called in the senior partner on the case if I assumed the meeting was about Peter, not about me. By arriving by myself, I made it clear that I knew they were interviewing me as a potential witness or suspect, rather than that I was meeting with them as one of Peter's lawyers. It was no wonder Rochon saw right through my feigned naïveté about why I was there alone.

Would I ever get any better at this? Of course, I might never have the chance to now. If Rochon put together a case against me as well, I might end up in prison for something I didn't do. Wouldn't that be ironic—top defense attorneys who'd successfully defended guilty clients unable to free their innocent daughter.

"I'm sorry," I said quietly.

He kicked back the Scotch rather than sipping it and poured himself another. Holy crap. That did not bode well.

He dropped into the chair on the other side of his desk. "You do understand the potential consequences of this, don't you? If they think there's even a remote chance they can make a conspiracy charge stick against you, they won't leave you walking free for us to use as a way to bring reasonable doubt into Peter's case. They'll try you both together."

Even if my parents could succeed in getting us acquitted, my reputation would be ruined. How could I go anywhere in public again, knowing people around me were speculating on whether I'd really helped my boyfriend kill his wife or not?

A piece of what my dad had said sunk in. "You'd wouldn't really use me to try to get Peter acquitted, would you?"

He gave me a look that said he was considering cursing again. "Of course not, but Rochon doesn't know that."

I swallowed, but it didn't ease the sandbox feeling in my mouth. I should have known better than to ask that question as well. As hard as he'd been on me, my dad had only ever wanted the best possible future for me. He wasn't above pulling strings and calling in favors to get it, so it was ludicrous to think he would ruin me to save Peter. I'd have an easier time believing he'd killed Eva Walsh to secure my future with Peter than that he'd harm me in any way.

I choked on my own spit and coughed. My dad frowned at me. I'd heard all the lectures about how rude it was to have a coughing fit in front of someone else, but I couldn't catch my breath.

My dad had a motive for killing Eva Walsh, and it didn't seem entirely crazy that he might have done it. For me. He'd fired and blackballed one of the most promising associates he'd ever had because the man was mocking me publicly. The poor guy could probably barely get a job flipping burgers after my dad was done with him.

But making sure a person had to move out of state if they wanted to work in their chosen field was still a far cry from killing someone.

My dad was no more a murderer than I was. Or than Peter was. I hoped. Pretty soon I was going to be so paranoid I'd have trouble figuring out who I could trust other than myself.

I put my feet back on the floor and tried to at least look like a grownup. "So what do we do to fix this?"

My dad slowly shook his head and drained the last sip of his second glass. "You're off the case, and I don't want you going anywhere near it. You're not to ask about it. You're not to access the files. Nothing. Do I make myself clear?"

I bit my lower lip and nodded. I'd blown my chance of helping Peter with one poorly-thought-out decision. Then again, even if I'd called my mom or dad right away, they'd still have taken me off the case. As soon as I became a suspect, either individually or in conjunction with Peter, they couldn't have me involved.

"And I don't want you to have any contact with Peter." He clunked his glass down on the table again and speared me to my chair with his gaze. "You've broken it off with him, haven't you?"

I squirmed in my seat. I had...sort of. I hadn't actually told Peter we were done.

The annoyingly honest part of my brain whispered that was because I wasn't sure yet whether I wanted us to be over. Yes, he'd concealed the fact that he was married. Yes, he should have told me and left his wife if he wanted to be with me. But maybe he'd made a mistake, too, and now he regretted it. Once this was all over and we'd—or, I should say, my parents had—proven him innocent, we might be able to work through this.

"Nicole?" My dad's voice was stern. "You have broken it off with him."

For now, at least, I guess I had no other choice. "Yes."

"Good. Since I don't want to risk any *misunderstandings*," he said the word in such a way that said what he really meant was *so that you can't claim you misunderstood later*, "when I say *no contact*, I mean I don't want you to see him or talk to him on the phone or in person. No email. No passing notes. No smoke signals."

I pursed my lips. Smoke signals. Seriously? "I got it."

"I don't know that you do. Do not have anything to do with Peter Walsh."

"I got it." I shoved to my feet. "Is there anything else?"

"I don't mean only until he's had his trial either."

That was odd. My dad had always seemed to like Peter and now he was going to be out of a job and we weren't supposed to see each other from this point on over something he didn't even do. "What does it matter after his trial's over?"

"Double jeopardy protects him if he's acquitted. It doesn't protect you."

He was right. Again. In other words, if I decided I eventually wanted a relationship with Peter, I still needed to figure out who really killed his wife. Even if I didn't want to be with Peter anymore, my future was on the line as well now. To clear my name, I needed to figure out who killed Eva Walsh.

And I had to do it without my dad's help, without access to any of the evidence the police or my parents found from this point on, and without either my dad or Rochon finding out.

I liked a challenge. I didn't like feeling as if I was about to scale Everest without an oxygen tank.

Chapter 7

My dad wasn't kidding about keeping me far away from the case. When I came in to work the next morning, I was exiled to filling out and filing paperwork like a legal assistant. Even more demeaning was that my dad had restricted my access to the case files. I found a sticky note in my dad's handwriting on my desk telling me that my password would no longer work if I tried to log in to any of the files on our internal servers related to Peter's case.

I guess I couldn't blame him. I *was* intending to secretly continue investigating the case, so his lack of faith in my promise to stay away could be considered cagey rather than insulting.

The second part of his plan must have been to keep me busy because the work that came my way all seemed to be time-sensitive. It was lunchtime before I even had a chance to stop long enough to think about Eva Walsh's murder.

I grabbed a quick salad from the deli around the corner—an attempt to offset all the comfort food I'd been inhaling the last two weeks since Peter was arrested—and scurried back to my office.

Someone had to have a motive to murder Eva Walsh. They also seemed to want to make sure Peter took the blame for it. That meant this could all be about taking revenge on Peter. So who had he wronged besides me?

I slowly munched a bite of cucumber. Criminal attorneys made enemies. Clients whose cases they'd lost, family of clients whose cases they'd lost, and victims or victims' families in cases they'd won could all hold a grudge. In the few minutes we'd had together, Peter had told me he'd seen an old client near his home. That lead seemed like as good a place to start as any.

The cases Peter handled prior to joining my parents' firm were in another state. It seemed less likely that an old client would track him across the country to take revenge, but to be thorough, I'd run an Internet search when I got home tonight.

The records of all the cases he'd been involved in since joining my parents' firm five years ago were stored in our computer system. I could easily narrow the search to cases he'd lost whose clients had also already been released.

I tapped my plastic fork on the edge of my takeout container. Problem was, if I logged in to those cases using my password, my dad might find out. The man was the type who left nothing up to chance. I wouldn't put it past him to have set up an alert on certain files that would activate with my password or to have attached a tracking pixel to my password.

If my password wasn't safe to use, I needed to swipe someone else's.

I poked the last cherry tomato around in my salad container. Only my parents had access to the section in the system where passwords were assigned and managed, and I was no computer hacker. Company policy was that we were supposed to memorize our passwords rather than writing them down. But there was one person I knew who wrote hers down anyway.

Carrie, one of our legal secretaries who was in her late fifties, had recently started to struggle with her memory. For about three weeks, she'd locked herself out of the system daily by going over the three login attempts the sign-in pages allowed. My mom quietly gave her special permission to write her password down as long as she kept it in her desk, out of sight.

I glanced at the clock. 12:50. Carrie would be back from lunch any minute. If I was doing this, I had to go now.

I tossed my fork and container into the trash and walked as casually as I could from my office and over to Carrie's desk. I'd watched her sneak a peek into her top right drawer when she needed to log in, so the password must be there.

The paper with the password on it had to stay put. If she "misplaced" it, my parents would cancel that password and assign her a new one immediately. I also didn't want to risk writing it down for myself. That could compromise the security of our system if I lost it and get me caught by my parents if they spotted it in my possession. So I had only a few seconds to memorize the password myself.

I acted like I was writing Carrie a note and eased her drawer open. The password lay inside on an index card—3PE8RPB4B.

My palms grew damp. Getting this wrong would also get me caught. I'd be using Carrie's company email address along with the password for login, and so if I failed, one of my parents would talk to her and they'd figure out someone other than Carrie had tried to use her password. Or they'd assume she'd forgotten and they'd assign her a new one. Either way, I wouldn't get what I needed, and I might get caught.

I needed a mnemonic. Something silly and easy to remember. It was how I managed my own password.

So what would work for Carrie's? Three purple elephants ate rhubarb pie before bed.

I double-checked it, slid the door closed, and walked away. Just before I reached my own office, I passed Carrie on her way back to her desk. She smiled and nodded on her way by.

My heart tripped over itself. I ducked into my office, closed the door, and slumped back against it. That was close.

Before my lunch hour ended, I logged in and jotted down Peter's clients who fit the profile. It was a short list, but I was out of time. I'd have to look for likely suspects in the list later.

Peter's neighborhood wasn't exactly on my way home from work...or in the same direction as my way home from work. But Peter would be out on bail any day now, and once he returned home, I'd be a fool to be spotted anywhere near his house. Before that happened, I wanted to talk to the neighbor who seemed to enjoy monitoring the neighborhood. Based on the addresses of the neighbors listed as witnesses, the two the police had recorded lived across the road and on the other side, so technically I wasn't interfering in the case, right? This neighbor wasn't even a witness to anything, according to the police.

I parked my car in nosy neighbor's driveway. In case I was being followed by either a police officer or someone hired by my dad, I wanted it to be clear that I wasn't going to Peter's house. Granted, what I *was* doing wasn't much better.

My finger had barely touched the doorbell when the door swung open.

The woman on the other side wasn't anything like what I'd imagined. I'd been picturing an elderly woman, gray hair, glasses, maybe even a shawl despite how the August heat had continued into September.

The woman who opened the door looked to be around my age. Certainly no older than her early thirties. She'd pulled her blonde hair back into a messy ponytail, and she wore yoga pants and a cute pink t-shirt with a smear of something carrot-orange on the shoulder.

I extended my hand. "I'm one of Peter Walsh's defense lawyers, and I was wondering if I could ask you a few questions."

She grabbed my hand, gave one shake, and then tugged. "Come on in."

I stumbled awkwardly after her. She didn't release my hand until I was safely inside and she'd shoved the door closed with her foot.

A nervous laugh sneaked out before I could catch it. I hadn't intended to go inside a stranger's house alone. "I have to admit that's not the sort of reception I'm used to."

"I'll let you in on a little secret." She put her hand up beside her mouth as if blocking her words from someone else, even though we were alone as far as I could tell. "I'd invite the mailman in if it meant some adult conversation." She made a follow-me gesture with her hand and headed off across the house. "Coffee? Tea? Juice? Milk?"

"I'm okay, thanks."

"Suit yourself." She walked backward for a second and smiled at me. "I need another cup of coffee."

I trailed after her through the living room and dodged my way around two playpens and a matching set of those jumpy chair things that babies seem to like. That, coupled with the *adult conversation* comment, pointed to a stay-at-home mom. Asking about it seemed like as good an ice breaker as any. "You have kids?"

She stepped aside to let me through the arched doorway and into the kitchen. She nodded in the direction of the counter. Two car seats butted up against the cupboards beneath the sink. Identical babies were still strapped into them, sound asleep.

She pulled a double-sized mug from the cupboard and motioned for me to take a seat at the table. "Don't get me wrong. I love that I have the chance to stay home with them for a while, but they're not exactly riveting conversationalists."

I settled in at the table. The window over the kitchen sink gave a clear view into their back yard, and by extension, of the fence surrounding the Walshes' back yard. "I didn't catch your name before. I'm Nicole."

"See. I told you. I'm forgetting how to talk to adults already." She emptied the coffee pot into her mug, measured out a fresh scoop of coffee, and set it percolating again. "I'm Monica Vankestren."

Monica flopped down into the chair across from me. "I figure you have about ten minutes max before the boys wake up, so I'd suggest you ask your questions quickly."

After she'd been so excited to invite me in, I'd hoped I'd have a chance to explore any hint of useful evidence she might provide about Peter and Eva and who might have visited them, but once again, I faced a ticking clock. "I'm sure you've heard on the news that Peter's been arrested for Eva's murder."

"That's not exactly a question." Monica smiled and sipped her coffee. Her eyes drifted closed for a moment. "Life would be so much easier if I could just install a caffeine drip straight into my blood stream."

I suddenly wished I'd accepted a cup of coffee so that I'd have something useful to do with my hands. If I wasn't officially off the case, I could have asked to record the conversation and then I would have had my phone to hold, but I didn't even have that. "So when you heard the news, was it unexpected?"

Arg. Now I was so thrown off my game that I couldn't even ask worthwhile questions.

But Monica nodded. "My husband and I both were. Or at least we were both surprised it was Eva. We were sure that if the police were called it would be because Peter and Dana finally went too far."

I twisted my hands in my lap under the table. Dana could be a man's name or a woman's name. Please let it not be another mistress. Please please please. "Who's Dana?"

"Eva's sister." Monica arched an eyebrow. "What kind of law firm are you guys that you haven't even looked into the family yet?"

"We like to start with the neighbors. Sometimes they know more about what's really happening than the family does."

Monica made a *hmm* noise and took another long slurp of her coffee.

"So Dana and Peter didn't get along?" I prompted. "Do you have any idea why?"

I couldn't see a reason why Dana would have killed Eva. She'd have been more likely to kill Peter if he was the one she didn't get along with. But if I might eventually need to talk to Dana, it would be good to know that she'd likely be unwilling to help anyone defending Peter and why there was hostility between them.

"I only know what I overheard. If Eva and Peter argued, they must have done it mostly inside where you couldn't hear them, but Dana'd scream at Peter right out in the driveway like no one was watching." Monica smirked. "I think she wanted to embarrass him."

I peeked at the babies in their car seats. Their heads still lolled to the side, mirror image lines of baby drool dribbling from their mouths, but it couldn't be too much longer now. "What did they usually fight about?"

Monica raised her mug again, glanced inside, frowned, and set it down. She looked back at the still-percolating coffeemaker and sighed. "Mostly Dana wanting Eva to leave Peter. Saying he only married her for the money. She knew he was cheating on her. Stuff like that."

Oh. Crap. What if Dana hired a private investigator to follow Peter? She'd have had her proof pretty quickly that he was cheating on Eva. With me. Assuming the PI took pictures, there was no way Dana was going to talk to me, and she was my best chance at finding out if there was anyone else who might have wanted Eva dead besides a former client of Peter's.

My throat seized up like drying concrete. And if she had proof of our affair and took it to Eva... "You said *if* Eva and Peter fought. You didn't hear any fights between them?"

Monica shook her head. "But I'm not outside much since the boys. I know Alice Reed, she lives across the street, she told me they were fighting just a couple of nights before Eva died." Her face was animated now, like the caffeine was kicking in at last. "Eva was waiting for Peter when he came home and lit into him right in the driveway like she was Dana. Peter hauled her inside before Alice or John could really make out what the fight was about." She rolled her eyes. "I'm surprised Dana wasn't in the driveway the next morning, threatening to move Eva out."

The first fight public enough the neighbors could hear but the protective sister didn't show up. What had changed?

One of the babies on the floor let out a howl loud enough that I was surprised the windows didn't rattle.

Monica swept her arms wide. "And that concludes the adult portion of the day. Can you see yourself out?"

"Sure." I skirted my way around the table. "One more thing real quick. Did you see anyone suspicious hanging around the neighborhood in the days leading up to Eva's death?"

Monica scooped the screaming baby from his car seat. His wails reached a decibel that made my ears ring, and his brother joined in.

She tucked the first one into one arm like a football and opened the fridge with her other hand. "There was the man with the shaved head in the beat-up car." She had to practically yell the words. "When he was still there by the time my husband came home from work, we called the police. The guy drove off when he spotted the police cruiser that they sent to check it out." She pulled back out of the fridge, a bottle in her hand. "I thought he might be casing the neighborhood, but do you think he had something to do with Eva's death?"

"That's what I'm hoping to find out."

Chapter 8

The three flights of stairs that I had to climb to reach my apartment—elevators made my heart ride up into my throat—felt like a single flight tonight. I had a solid lead on who might have killed Eva Walsh, and I'd found a package waiting for me from my Uncle Stan.

As soon as I had the door locked behind me, I turned on my laptop to start trying to find pictures to match the names on my list of Peter's clients and then grabbed a pair of scissors.

The package was heavy and marked FRAGILE. I sliced away the packing tape. Inside nestled a glass bottle of rich brown maple syrup. A handwritten note was rubber-banded to the bottle.

From my own trees, to help ease your sweet tooth. I'm proud of you. Give me a call when you have a chance.

Love, Uncle Stan

I stroked my fingers down the side of the bottle. Despite my dad's refusal to speak to Uncle Stan since my uncle quite his lucrative cardiology practice to purchase a maple syrup farm in Michigan, Uncle Stan and I spoke and emailed every week.

Or at least we usually did. I'd been less than communicative since I found out Peter was married. I'd sent Uncle Stan a quick email to tell him what happened, but then I'd avoided calling him. He understood me better than my own parents did, and I couldn't bear the thought that he might be disappointed in me, too.

I'm proud of you, he'd written.

He might as well have written *I know why you haven't called. You don't need to worry.*

I'd give him a call tomorrow. Reading his note, it was clear I'd been silly not to call.

For now, I needed to match a name to a face and make myself something to eat. It was after eight o'clock, and my whole body felt shaky and weak. I grabbed an apple to hold me over and settled into my chair.

The first client whose name I checked fit Monica's description. He'd been sentenced to five years for dealing drugs, but he could have easily been paroled before serving the full sentence.

I searched the other names to be safe, but none of them had shaved heads. While they might have changed their appearance, the more reasonable explanation seemed to be that the man who matched the description was the man Monica saw.

I tossed the apple core at my garbage, missed, and hopped up to put it in. The next problem I needed to tackle was how to give this information to my dad without revealing that I'd openly disobeyed him. If I had to, I'd face his wrath, but I'd rather avoid it. And I had to pass it along to my dad if it was going to do Peter any good. No way was I traipsing off to talk to an ex-con potential murderer on my own.

Dad had taken me off the case only last night, and he'd kept me busy all day today, as well as locking me out of Peter's files. So it didn't seem like an unbelievable stretch to tell him this was information I'd dug up before he removed me from the case.

I clicked open my email program, wrote him a quick message with the name of Peter's former client, and recommended he ask Peter about it.

Then I shut everything down. With Uncle Stan's gift, I'd developed a craving for French toast, and it'd be a quick, easy meal to make. I crossed my fingers and peeked into the fridge.

Bread and milk but no eggs.

I snagged my purse from where I'd dropped it on the counter. With any luck, I'd make the grocery store before it closed.

By the time I returned to my apartment, the streetlights bathed the world in a yellowish haze, and the hot-asphalt smell had left the air.

I tucked the container of eggs under my arm and shifted my keys to that hand so I could punch in the door code to my building.

A hand grabbed my shoulder.

My heart plunged into a death spiral, and I screeched, dropping my eggs and spinning around, my keys between my fingers like a weapon. All the self-defense classes I'd taken at my gym had my other arm up instinctively to block any blow that might come.

"Jeez, Nicole." Peter's face came into focus. "It's just me."

I lowered my hands, and my heart rate slowed somewhat, though my blood still surged through my veins, making me feel a little like I'd downed a double-shot espresso. "What are you doing here?"

"Your dad told me the police found out about our relationship. Now that they know, there's no reason to avoid each other anymore." Peter pointed toward my feet. "You dropped something."

I stooped and picked up my egg carton. The bottom felt gooey. I popped the lid. All but three of the eggs had smashed. I bit back a sigh. Three was better than nothing. Maybe I could even try filtering the egg shell shards out of the others. "Eggs. I was going to make French toast."

He flashed me the smile I used to find irresistibly charming—the one that crinkled his eyes slightly at the corners and added a devil-may-care aura to his normally solemn appearance. "I could join you." He stroked my hair back from my face, his knuckles grazing my skin. "I've missed you."

Instead of the heat his touch normally burned into my belly, a tiny shiver ran over my skin. And not the good kind. He'd been avoiding me because he wanted to hide our relationship from the police, and he didn't seem to have considered that I might have been keeping my distance for an entirely different reason. Like I might not want to keep dating someone who'd lied to me about something as major as whether or not he was already married.

I stepped back out of his reach. "You still shouldn't be here. How would it look for you to be seen going into my apartment when you're supposed to be grieving your dead *wife*?"

He stiffened and the hand he'd caressed my face with a moment before clenched at his side. "Are we going to do this again? I told you I never meant to hurt you."

"Again? The short conversation we had in the police station doesn't count as an apology." Maybe Ahanti and my dad were right, even if their reasons for wanting me to stay away from Peter were different. Maybe I would be an idiot if I took him back. I couldn't exactly cross my arms the way I wanted to with a leaking carton of eggs clutched in one hand, so I planted my free hand on my hip. "Or an explanation."

He closed the space between us and wrapped a hand gently around the back of my neck, under my hair. He leaned close and trailed a kiss along the edge of my jaw, onto my ear.

"Can't we go inside and talk about this?" he whispered. "I'll make it up to you. I promise."

Was this how he'd kept me from asking questions before? I tried to replay in my mind times when I'd asked questions that could have led me to discovering his secret life. They'd always been followed up with some distraction that felt perfectly natural at the time. I guess I'd learned something about myself at least from all this.

I pressed my eggless hand into his chest. "If you don't take a step back, I'm going to plant my knee in your groin."

He let me go and cursed softly. "You want an explanation?"

I nodded.

"Fine." Peter glanced back over his shoulder as if suddenly nervous someone else might overhear. "Eva and I married young, and she paid my way through school. After someone does something like that for you, it's not as easy to leave them as you'd think, even if you don't love them anymore."

It felt surreal hearing the story now, when I knew how it ended. I studied his face and body language. If he was lying to me again, I wanted to catch it this time. Assuming he wasn't such a good liar that I'd never see it no matter how long and hard I looked.

"When I met you, I realized that what I felt for Eva wasn't love. It was gratitude. But I liked the lifestyle we lived, and her money was what made that possible. Her trust fund."

The air I'd been holding in left my body in a rush, and a queasy feeling filled my stomach. He loved his wife's money more than he loved me.

The pride I'd inherited from my father forced me to straighten my shoulders and not let it show how his words were corroding me inside. "Did she know about us?"

He hesitated a second too long. A tingle traced the back of my neck.

"Eventually." He looked to the side. "She didn't want a divorce any more than I did, so we decided not to get one."

The hesitation could mean he didn't want to tell me the truth but gave me the truth anyway, or it could mean he'd lied to me again. I couldn't tell with Peter.

Hearing it from him let me see the situation through the perspective of the police, though. A husband who wanted his wife's money but no longer wanted his wife had a good motive for murder. Peter claimed he and Eva had decided to stay together and that he hadn't killed her, but what benefit would there have been for Eva in staying with a man who didn't love her anymore? It tasted like a lie, like biting into a piece of fruit on the edge of going bad.

"You know how this sounds, don't you?" I said.

"Why do you think I didn't want to tell you?" He held out his hand, palm forward like he was taking an oath in court. "But I swear to you that I didn't kill her. And that I loved you—love you. I want us to be together, even if that means waiting until this is all over because of the way it would look to the police."

He reached for my hand, and I blocked him with my leaking egg carton.

Perhaps he was innocent. Perhaps he was just a self-centered jerk. Perhaps he loved me.

But perhaps everything I'd loved about him was an act. And perhaps he'd masterfully manipulated all of us to achieve his goals. And perhaps he'd killed Eva.

For the first time since I saw that newscast, I wasn't confident in Peter's innocence. Peter was a master manipulator and a user. And up until now, I'd fallen for it.

I punched in the door code and it buzzed open. "I'll think about what you said, but for now, you need to stay away from me."

I shoved the door shut behind me so he couldn't follow, and I didn't look back.

I had to find out the truth, whether I liked what I discovered or not. Because regardless of what my dad said, the truth mattered.

Chapter 9

Figuring out what happened to Eva Walsh meant I needed to speak to the person who knew the most about Eva and Peter's relationship—Eva's sister Dana.

The next morning, as soon as I'd showered, I called in sick to work. My parents would guess I wasn't sick, but they couldn't prove it, and I knew neither of them would take the time off to check on me.

Then I looked up the number for Eva Walsh's sister (it was easy enough to get her name from Eva's obituary), and convinced her that she was legally obligated to speak to Peter's defense counsel. Her tone suggested she suspected I was lying since the lawyer who called her before hadn't said anything about it, but I threw around a few legal terms and she agreed to meet me at the Reflecting Pool in front of the Washington Monument on her coffee break.

Instead of driving, I took the Metro. I wasn't in the mood to fight traffic or hunt for parking, and if I was being honest with myself, my mind wasn't focused enough to drive. The last thing I needed right now was an accident.

I reached downtown with plenty of time to spare, so I took the path leading off from the Lincoln Memorial and the Reflecting Pool to the Vietnam Women's Memorial. Of all the memorials and monuments in DC, this one had always been my favorite.

Today, the statue was abnormally free of the tourist crowd that usually scrambled all over it, taking pictures, so I moved in close. A uniformed woman held a fallen soldier across her lap. She gazed down at him, one arm behind his shoulder and a hand pressed to his chest, but it was clear the life was gone from him.

It was a sad image, but it also spoke to courage. They were women willing to take risks and make sacrifices for the sake of others. They were what I wanted to be but wasn't.

I made my way back toward the Washington Monument, walking alongside the Reflecting Pool so I could watch the geese paddling around in it. I reached the end at the same time as a woman with a storkish quality—skinny and all legs—and Eva Walsh's high cheekbones. It had to be Dana.

She glanced down at her watch. When she looked up again, our gazes met.

She shook her head and backed up. "I know who you are. I'm not talking to you even if it is the law."

That answered the question of whether she'd hired a private investigator and whether he'd taken pictures of Peter and his mistress—me. Time to drop the pretense. "It's not the law. But I'm also not here in the capacity of Peter's defense attorney."

"Uh huh." She pivoted on her heel and marched off across the grass.

I scurried after her. Her taller frame and longer legs meant I practically had to jog to keep up. "Peter lied to me, too. I didn't know about Eva until after she died. And I'm tired of not knowing what's the truth and what isn't."

Dana let out a string of words describing Peter that would have made a convict's ears burn. "You're not the first." Dana stopped and swiveled to face me. "You're just the first one I could prove."

I stumbled over my own feet, and she grabbed my arm, steadying me. I smiled at her in thanks, but it felt like trying to press my hand into drying cement. "You're sure?"

She rolled her eyes. "Honestly, you and Eva. I don't see what it is about him that makes it so hard to believe." She poked me in the shoulder with her index and middle fingers hard enough to leave a bruise. "He doesn't deserve that kind of loyalty."

I instinctively rubbed the spot she'd jabbed. I knew exactly what it was about Peter. When you were with him, you felt like the only woman who existed. You certainly felt like the most interesting, intelligent one because of the way he wanted to talk about you rather than about himself and how he always asked for your opinions. You didn't want any of that to be a lie because, if it was, you weren't special—you were gullible and naïve.

In hindsight, I could see all of it in a different light. Talking about me also made sure that I didn't dig too deeply into his life, and asking for my opinion on topics ensured that he could portray himself as my perfect match.

Instead of saying all that, I said, "It's hard to explain. But what I want now is the truth. Will you help me?"

Dana's expression softened, the crinkles around her eyes looking more like wrinkles. She had to be the older sister. "Eva said that same thing to me the last time I saw her. *Will you help me?*"

Dana twisted a ring around on her finger. At first I thought it was a piece of gaudy costume jewelry. The clashing lime-green and orange stones rested next to each other in the pattern of two interlinked circles in a gold setting.

Then I recognized it. It was one of the sister rings I'd seen advertised everywhere over the summer.

I nodded toward her hand. "Topaz and citrine, right? For your birthdays."

Dana stopped twisting the ring and blinked rapidly. "You won't like the truth any more than Eva did, but maybe I can save you since I couldn't save her." She slid her phone out of her purse. "Lemme call my boss and tell him I won't be back. He won't give me crap if I tell him it's about Eva's murder."

We found a spot on the green to sit where no one else was close enough to hear our conversation. Dana dropped right onto the grass, skirt notwithstanding, and tucked her legs up under her. I had to envy that kind of flexibility.

"Eva had just turned eighteen when she met Peter. He was twenty-two, maybe twenty-three, at the time. She was volunteering at a food bank, and she started coming home with stories about this guy who worked there as a janitor, how he'd been telling her about how jealous he was that she was attending college. He fed her these lines about how he wanted to go to law school, but he'd never be able to afford it."

I folded my hands in my lap and stayed quiet. I'd assumed Peter grew up in a privileged home the way I did and the way Eva obviously had.

"Our parents didn't realize she was falling for him. I saw it, but I was dealing with too much of my own sh...stuff"—she glanced my way with a look on her face that said she'd noticed me cringe at her colorful description of Peter earlier—"at the time to be a big sister the way I should have. She eloped with him before her nineteenth birthday."

The family dynamics clarified in my mind. Dana had likely been the unconventional, rebellious child, closely monitored through her teenage years to make sure she didn't make a decision she'd regret for the rest of her life. It'd probably come as a horrible shock to their parents that Eva had been the one to end up in trouble. But Dana's tendency to walk the line had made her savvy, and good girl Eva didn't have the training to spot a con man before it was too late.

Maybe Eva and I weren't as different as I'd once thought.

Dana brushed her bangs back off her forehead and fanned her face. "Our parents controlled the trust funds they'd set up for us. They could take them away, I guess you'd say, any time before our twenty-fifth birthdays. When Eva and Peter showed back up talking about putting him through college and then law school by dipping in to her trust fund, my parents demanded they sign a post-nup or they'd never see a penny of the money. They signed."

The sun beating down on us was sure to leave me boiled-lobster red, but I fought against a shiver. "He never mentioned the post-nup, even when I was still on his case."

Dana snorted. "Peter doesn't mention a lot of things. He's a master at controlling information." Her shoulders slumped slightly. "And people. After they signed the post-nup, Peter convinced Eva that they should travel first, while they were young. She didn't think it was a good idea, but she loved him, so she dropped out of school and they went."

I had a pretty good guess where the story was headed. "Your parents had to threaten to deny them access to the trust fund before he finally went to school, didn't they?"

Dana tapped her nose. "My parents waited for two years, hoping they'd 'get it out of their systems and settle down.'" Her voice carried a bitter tinge. "Believe me, I never got as many chances. They yanked my trust fund and never gave it back long before I hit twenty-five."

Who would inherit Eva's money if Peter were convicted of her murder? Legally, he wouldn't be allowed to benefit from his crime, which meant he couldn't inherit or claim Eva's life insurance policy if the court declared him guilty. Eva's obituary mentioned that her parents had predeceased her. If Dana were next in line...well, people had murdered family members for a lot less. And as Eva's sister, she might even have a key to the house. That gave her motive and opportunity.

The problem with that theory was Dana seemed to genuinely hate Peter. Hatred that deep had to stem from a genuine love for her sister. Then again, as I'd recently learned, some people could fake emotions.

I had to ask the question. "If Peter's found guilty, who inherits the money now?"

Dana's eyes narrowed slightly. "Not me, if that's what you're asking. If they'd had a kid, it'd be held in trust for them. Since they don't, it'll go to our cousin down in Florida. She's only sixteen, so I'm pretty sure she didn't kill Eva, either."

Her goodwill seemed to be evaporating in the heat after that question. My throat had gone drier than even the hot day merited. "I'm sorry, but I had to ask."

Her lips took on an *mmm-hmm* expression.

"I'm looking for the truth, remember? I can't assume anything anymore."

The sarcasm in her expression bled away. "Yeah. I guess so."

I still had a lot more I wanted to know, and I'd almost lost my best source. The safest path seemed to be to lead her back into doing most of the talking. "So Peter went to school and they stayed married."

"Of course they stayed married. Peter loved Eva's trust fund."

Peter had said as much to me, though coming from him it'd sounded more like the reason he stayed was gratitude rather than greed. I felt like I should say something in response, but my mind was blank. "I see."

"Once she turned twenty-five and our parents handed over control, Peter and Eva fought constantly about it. Peter wanted them to quit work and enjoy their lives. Eva'd grown up. She wanted to do some good in the world. I started to suspect he was stashing away money so that he wouldn't need her one day, and

I was certain he was cheating on her. I finally hired a PI to prove it."

I'd suspected the private investigator after my talk with Monica, but this was the first I'd heard about Peter basically embezzling money from his wife. "Did you find any evidence that he was stealing from her trust fund?"

Dana shook her head. "Once I found proof of his cheating, I didn't need to. I showed Eva the pictures, gave her the number of a divorce lawyer, and sat with her while she called. That was a couple of days before she died."

I sucked in air. Peter definitely hadn't told us Eva had hired a divorce lawyer. In fact, he'd told me last night that they'd decided to stay married. "You're sure? Do you know if she told him she was filling for divorce?"

"I don't know." Dana pushed her bangs back again and held them back this time. She dabbed her forehead with a tissue. "That was the last time I talked to her. I told her I'd help her move out, but she said her money bought the house. If anyone was leaving, it was him and that she wasn't going to back down this time."

That could explain the fight the neighbors heard. A weight settled in my chest, tight and hot, like I had a sunburn on the inside. It also gave Peter an even stronger motive for wanting Eva dead.

Dana hopped to her feet. The movement looked more graceful than someone who'd been sitting on their legs for a half hour should have. "I don't feel like talking about this anymore. I've told you everything I told the police now anyway. It's all I know, and I really need a drink."

I struggled to a standing position. One of my feet was asleep and threatened to give out under me. I wiggled it. "I just have two more questions." Dana frowned, but I held up my hand. "They're quick. I promise."

She nodded slowly.

I swished a finger across the screen of my phone and pulled up the phone number that called Eva's cell the morning of her death. My instincts said whoever made that call had also been involved with setting up Eva's death. "Do you know who this number belongs to?"

I held it out to Dana. And then I watched her for even the slightest reaction.

Dana peered closely at the phone and her brow furrowed. "I don't. What does this have to do with Eva and Peter?"

No facial tics. No hesitation. No sign at all that she might have recognized the number.

I slid the phone back into my purse. "Probably nothing at all. One more thing. Eva's cell phone case." The question jammed up behind my tongue and didn't want to come out. The theory forming in my mind pointed directly at Peter. "Was it cracked the day you last saw her?"

Dana snorted again. I'm sure her parents loved that quirk as much as mine would. "Are you kidding me? No way would Eva have kept a cracked cell phone cover. Half my clothes come from stuff she was going to give away because she scuffed a shoe or spotted a lose thread."

I extended my hand, but it felt like someone else was in control of my body. If Eva would have replaced a cracked cell phone case immediately, then the most likely time for it to have cracked was the morning of her death. I knew from the police reports that the only prints on Eva's cell phone belonged to Eva and Peter.

"Thanks for your help," I said, manners on autopilot.

She took my hand and squeezed. Hard. "I know you think you wanted the truth, but I've watched Peter work for over a decade. Don't even give him a chance to talk to you. He's a born con man."

She walked away before I had a chance to figure out an answer.

But she was right. Peter had been controlling this case the whole time, and he might have even manipulated me into providing enough reasonable doubt to get him acquitted of a crime I was now almost sure he did, in fact, commit.

Chapter 10

I'm not sure how long I sat on the green after Dana left, but the way my skin turned from whitish to red suggested it was longer than I realized. I knew what I needed to do. I needed to go to my dad, lay out my theory about what really happened, and try to convince him to talk Peter into a plea deal. There was still time.

There had to still be time. Because I knew what would happen if they went to trial. I'd done a decent job of making sure my dad had the means to provide reasonable doubt, and no one was better at wooing a jury than my dad. He'd gotten other clients acquitted on less.

I practiced what I wanted to say during the whole Metro ride, even though I'd likely forget it all the minute I had to face my dad. The act at least helped calm me down rather than pushing me to continue to seriously consider hyperventilating into the abandoned paper bag in the seat next to mine.

I nearly bumped into Carrie on my way into the office.

She sidestepped out of my way. "Nicole! What are you doing here? You don't look well enough to be back at work yet."

That was encouraging. I really must look awful if Carrie believed my story about being sick today. At least that would work in my favor with the rest of the office, and no one would suspect I'd been out today for less legitimate reasons.

I smoothed a hand over my hair. "I needed to talk to my dad about something, and you know how hard it is to get him on the phone."

Carrie patted my shoulder in a motherly way. "Well, you go home and get some more rest after, okay?"

It was enough to make me wish I hadn't stolen her password.

I knocked on my dad's office door. He opened it and held up a finger, his cell phone in hand, his earpiece on. He swept me from head to toe in a single glance and frowned. He, clearly, wasn't as easily fooled as Carrie was.

He pointed a stiff finger at the chair in front of his desk and closed his door with more force than was necessary.

"Let me give you a call back," he said to the person on the other end of the phone call.

He slid his cell phone onto his buffed and polished desk, dropped the earpiece beside it, and sat in the chair behind the desk rather in the chair right beside me. "You look the same way you did the one time you brought home a B on a test."

I felt about the same, too, my stomach so knotted up I might need to make a dash for the trash can on the floor in the corner. He wasn't going to like what I had to say now even less than he'd liked that one and only B. And that one and only B had gotten me grounded for a month.

"I know I'm off Peter's case, but I've been looking into it a little more anyway." I blurted the words out so rapidly I wasn't sure they were even coherent.

My dad leaned back and crossed him arms over his chest—his classic stance. "I know. Your excuse of having found that information about Peter's former client prior to being taken off the case was flimsy at best."

I should have known he wouldn't buy my excuse. He was one of the best investigators alive. Which left one question. "If you knew...?"

"Why didn't you receive an angry phone call from me?"

Heat built under my collar and I nodded.

"The information will be useful in building our defense."

His face remained austere, but his tone was almost...proud. I could feel my determination dripping away. I dropped my gaze to the floor, half expecting to see it pooling there.

Maybe I couldn't go through with this after all.

Maybe I could keep that tone of voice cradled away in my heart, feeding off of it for years.

"You look like you still have more to confess," my dad said.

I ground my toe into the floor, and a spear of self-hatred tried to chisel its way into my heart. Even that wasn't enough to convince me to sacrifice that tone of pride.

Perhaps I wouldn't have to. The one part of me that ever managed to make my dad proud was my detail skills. I'd often managed to put pieces together that other people missed. I could do that now, laying it out to him like something I wanted his feedback on rather than like a conclusion I'd already reached.

"Not confess." I picked my words carefully. "But I noticed a few things about Peter's case that could be a problem, and I wanted to run them by you."

He eyed his phone. "Will this take long? I have to return the call I was on within the next half hour, before they close for the weekend."

"It won't take that long."

He gave me the go-ahead nod.

I'd only get one chance at this. I had to make myself clear the first time. "I noticed that some of the evidence could give the prosecution a strong case."

My dad's face remained impassive, but I wanted to kick myself as soon as the words were out. This was why I floundered when arguing a case. Obviously some of the evidence gave the prosecution a strong case or they wouldn't have charged Peter in the first place.

I shifted position, but the chair seemed suddenly hard and pokey beneath me. "What I mean is that a case could be made that Peter attempted to make Eva's death look like an accident and failed. That her death was premeditated."

A little feedback would be nice, but he continued to wait.

"Eva Walsh swam every morning before work in the summer months, so Peter bought a burner phone and used it to call her cell phone that morning after he saw her climb into the pool. He knew that if he claimed she slipped while running for her cell phone, the police would check to see if a call actually came in." I could hear the pitch of my voice start to rise. I took a long breath and started again. "Eva did climb out of the pool to take the call, but her cell phone was on the poolside table, not inside. When she climbed out, Peter attacked her, smashing her head..."

My voice cracked this time. My dad raised a disdainful eyebrow and his gaze wandered away toward his phone. I straightened in my seat.

"Smashing her head into the concrete." I added force to my words, and his gaze came back to me. "Knocking over the poolside table in the process and cracking her cell phone case when it hit the hard surface of the pool deck. Eva Walsh never kept any item that was damaged. If her cell phone case had been cracked the day before, she would have already replaced it. It had to have been damaged during her struggle with Peter. He put it on the kitchen counter afterward to corroborate his story."

"And why would he have killed her?" my dad asked, his voice soft, almost like he was prompting a student.

I'd so rarely heard that tone of patience from him that I wasn't sure whether it meant he was following me and believing me or whether it meant something else entirely. "Eva found out about her husband's affair two days before her death. She'd called a divorce lawyer and planned to leave him. Due to their post-nuptial agreement, Peter would have been left with nothing if she divorced him."

My dad smiled, a full-bodied, well-done smile. "Now why can't you handle opening and closing arguments that well in front of an actual judge and jury?"

The smile took almost all the sting out of the words. Why couldn't I indeed. Surely my father was more intimidating than a room full of strangers. But we both knew better. As soon as I went from talking to one person to talking to many, I fell apart.

The warmth from his smile suddenly seemed to bounce off an invisible wall between us. "I don't know."

He didn't break eye contact. We sat quietly for one heartbeat. Two.

I forced myself to hold his gaze and swallowed to moisten my spastically closing throat. It was now or never. "What would we do if that seemed like the most logical explanation for what happened?"

"We'd make sure we knew how to poke holes in the argument and cast enough reasonable doubt to have our client acquitted anyway."

It was the firm set of his lips, the challenge in his eyes, the way he leaned back casually in his chair, body relaxed—he wasn't surprised by what I'd told him. He already knew it. He knew Peter was guilty.

He'd known all along.

Chapter 11

The last piece of me that wanted to cling to the belief that I had it wrong and that Peter was innocent died.

Blood rushed into my head so fast the room seemed to tilt on its axis for a minute. I couldn't hyperventilate here, in front of my dad. *Pull it together, Nicole. You're stronger than this.* "You knew."

My dad slid the earpiece back on. "Go home, Nicole. You're not well enough to be in at work today, remember?"

I could feel something inside me cracking in time to the blood pounding in my ears. I slowly stood and stepped toward his desk rather than away from it. "How could you?"

The words came out in a hiss rather than the scream I felt inside. How could he still defend Peter knowing he'd bashed his wife's head into the concrete exactly like the police said? How could he still defend him knowing it was premeditated rather than a momentary lapse in judgment? How could he still defend him knowing that his only daughter had likely been Peter's next pawn?

He came to his feet as well, never one to have to look up to anyone. "How could I what?"

The feigned tone of innocence felt like sandpaper across my soul. "You know what. He killed her. He lied."

His upper lip twitched. In a man with less self-control, it might have turned into a full lip curl, but instead it was there and gone. "The law has no room for emotion. You need to learn how to manage yours or you'll never be anything more than a second-rate lawyer."

I leaned heavily on the desk. Maybe that's why I fit here about as well as a giraffe in a pup tent. I couldn't take the emotion out. I couldn't see the people who'd died as another fact in a case. And I couldn't pretend like guilt and innocence didn't matter. "I don't understand how it doesn't bother you that he's guilty."

He shook his head, strode to the door, and held it open. "They're always guilty."

As I came out of our office building, I walked in the direction of my apartment building even though it would take me over an hour to get there on foot. The Metro would be packed this time of day, and I needed to be alone.

I yanked my cell phone out and punched in Uncle Stan's number. Then I prayed to whatever higher power might be out there listening that he'd be available to answer.

"Have you figured out who did it yet?" Uncle Stan's voice said on the other end of the line.

He couldn't mean the case with Peter. I hadn't told him I was trying to find the real killer. "What?"

"The new mystery I sent you. This one's obvious. I thought you might be calling to say you'd figured it out already."

That made more sense. Uncle Stan and I read mysteries together and competed to see who could solve the crime the earliest. We wrote down our guesses after finishing each chapter so there wasn't any cheating, accidental or intentional. I'd seen the latest gifted ebook come in to my inbox yesterday, but I hadn't gotten a chance to download it yet.

I let my shoulders slump. I'd held them rebar-straight the whole time I'd been with my dad, and muscle spasms sent splinters of pain all down my back. "I've been too busy trying to solve a real crime."

And that's when I lost it. It was a good thing no one was around other than the cars speeding by because tears streamed down my face, and I had nothing except my t-shirt sleeves to sop them up with.

The whole time I cried, Uncle Stan murmured in my ear that it was going to be okay, whatever had happened, we'd figure out a way to handle it, and that he could be on a plane tonight if I needed him.

All of it only made me cry harder because he said everything I hadn't realized I'd wanted my dad to say.

When I got control of myself again, I told Uncle Stan everything that had happened, including what I'd figured out. My confession probably walked the line of legality, but I wasn't technically Peter's lawyer anymore, and none of what I said had been told to me when I was bound by lawyer–client confidentiality.

"You need to go to the police, Nikki," Uncle Stan said when I finished.

I'd thought about that. "I don't have any solid evidence. The chip from the back of her phone is inadmissible now because they've already cleared the scene. And even if it could be used as evidence, it still doesn't prove anything." I scrubbed the last tears off my cheeks. "He's going to get away with it unless I can find a way to prove he did it. I even helped them unintentionally by providing alternative suspects."

"You said the prosecutor has all the evidence you have. They might still be able to make a strong enough case for a jury to convict Peter."

I shook my head, then remembered he couldn't see me. "You know that's a long shot with Dad as defense counsel. And Peter's smart. He's planned this all out. He almost made the accident ploy believable." I'd believed it, after all.

"No one's perfect. Not your dad. Not Peter."

True enough. I just didn't see where the gaps might be. It felt like I'd chased down every possible avenue when I was trying to prove Peter innocent. "The only missing piece is the burner cell phone, and that could be anywhere."

Though maybe not. I stopped and watched the cars zip by, jockeying for position as if one car length's difference would actually help them reach their destination any faster.

Peter wouldn't have had much time. After making the phone call, he would have had minutes at most to kill Eva, toss her in the water, put her cell phone on the kitchen counter, haul her back out of the pool to make it look believable, and also hide the burner phone. His timeline had probably been accelerated because the neighbor heard Eva scream and came rushing over.

"Nicole? Are you still there?"

"Sorry, yes." I continued my trek home. My feet ached. This was the farthest I'd walked in my whole life, and I guessed I still had halfway to go. "I was thinking that Peter would have had to hide the phone someplace close by. He didn't have time to dispose of it properly, and if the police missed it in their initial search, he might feel confident enough to have left it wherever he stashed it."

"Is that information you could bring to the police?"

Captain Rochon and his team had more years of experience than I did. No doubt they'd already questioned the location of the burner phone. Not finding it was a major hole in their case, one I'm sure my dad and Peter had some secret plan to exploit.

"The police can't go back into Peter's home and search it again. It's the same problem as with the chip from her cell phone case. And if Peter somehow hid it outside of the search perimeter, even if I found it, there would be chain of custody issues."

Assuming, of course, that if I brought in the phone, I could convince them that I hadn't been a part of it and hiding the phone all along. But that phone seemed to be the only hope of making sure Peter was punished for what he'd done to his wife.

"If you found it?" For a second, the accusatory tone to his words eerily echoed my father. It wasn't often they sounded like brothers. "Tell me you're not thinking about going anywhere near that man's house."

"Of course not," I answered instinctively.

The words tasted sour coming out. It might have been the first time I'd ever lied to my Uncle Stan.

Chapter 12

I turned the conversation away from Peter's case after that. Before we ended the call, Uncle Stan cautioned me again to stay away from Peter—advice I was becoming all too familiar with.

Advice I planned to follow as soon as I found that burner phone. I could get into Peter's home and snoop around. The police couldn't.

Once I found the phone, the police might be able to get special dispensation from a judge to include the burner phone into evidence if I carefully recorded where I'd found it. Even if a judge turned them down, the police could use the phone to try to trace where it'd been purchased. They might get lucky and find security camera footage of Peter buying it. I wanted to think he might have been cocky enough to pay with a credit card, but that wasn't likely. He'd have known that the police would check his credit card history.

I stopped my walk in the parking lot of a shopping center and called for a cab.

While I was waiting for it to arrive, I dialed Peter.

"Hey, babe," he answered. "Does this mean you've decided it's time to make up?"

The names that went through my head for him were only a slightly more polite version of what Dana called him earlier. "I was thinking we could get together tonight. It's about time I saw your house."

I added a flirty tone to my voice. I couldn't flirt when I actually wanted to, but I could act. I knew how to play a witness, and that's all Peter was to me now.

He chuckled, and bile burned my throat. "Why don't you swing by around 7:30? There's an outdoor concert in the park near my house. We should be able to hear it from the back yard. We can sit outside and sip some wine."

My brain did a nose dive over all the things that were horribly, horribly wrong with that offer.

I wanted to say, *I don't drink, you self-absorbed jerk.*

I wanted to say, *Shall I put my deck chair over the stain you left on the concrete patio when you murdered your wife, or would you like that prime spot?*

But what I actually said was, "Sounds good. I'll see you then."

As soon as the door closed behind me at Peter's house, he pinned me against the wall, his lips greedy on mine, his hands roaming. My heart beat against my rib cage like it wanted to escape. I wanted to escape along with it.

But I couldn't because, if the burner phone was hidden anywhere, it was here. I tried to generate a moderately believable response, a daydream of scrubbing my skin off playing through my mind.

Peter pulled back. "You okay?"

I swallowed down the lump in my throat. "Just tired and hungry. I haven't had anything to eat since breakfast."

He grinned, and for the first time, it looked smarmy to me. "That's an easy enough problem to solve."

He'd laid out a spread of crackers, cheese, and fruit, alongside a bottle of white wine. Outside, citronella candles flickered all around the pool and in a semicircle around two lounge chairs. It would have been romantic two months ago, before I knew what had happened only a foot or two away.

"Let's take this outside." He balanced the platter on one hand and snagged the wine bottle in the other. "The concert should be starting by now." He nodded toward a cupboard near the door. "Grab us a couple of glasses?"

I headed for the cupboard and took my time selecting two glasses. Somehow I'd need to figure out a way to get Peter out of the backyard long enough for me to look around. To search inside, I could make some excuse about needing to use the restroom.

Peter opened the door, and the sound of a big band playing a piece of music from *The Majestic* rolled in. I recognized it because it was the one movie starring Jim Carrey that I liked. Peter shut the door behind him, and silence descended on the kitchen again.

The wine glass I'd pulled from the shelves slipped from my fingers and shattered on the counter.

The glass in the door was soundproof.

That was why I hadn't heard Ahanti when she called for me. It wasn't that I'd been preoccupied. That was why the neighbors never seemed to hear Peter and Eva fight. It wasn't that they weren't fighting.

There was no way Eva could have heard her phone ring through soundproof glass, and there was no way Peter could have heard her phone ring outside through soundproof glass. The police wouldn't have realized that the unbreakable evidence they needed was in the door itself.

The glass door slid open again and Peter stuck his head back in. "You coming?"

His gaze flickered to the glass shards spewed across the granite counter, the stem of the wine glass still rocking slightly back and forth, the only piece left partly whole.

He stepped inside, his eyebrows drawn down. "What happened?"

"Low blood sugar." Oh good lord, my voice sounded borderline hysterical. Fortunately, he'd probably assume it was because I broke one of his glasses. "It slipped right out of my hand."

His eyebrows kept that pinched look, but he walked over and turned me toward the door. "I didn't realize you were *that* hungry. Go outside and eat something. I'll clean this up and get the glasses."

I scuttled outside and shoved two pieces of cheese into my mouth in case he was watching me. They choked me on the way down, and I hacked.

My phone vibrated, and Ahanti's name blinked onto the screen. I'd let it go to voicemail. She was sure to ask where I was, and I didn't have time to explain...or be lectured.

I glanced back in Peter's direction. He wasn't there anymore, which probably meant he'd gone to get a broom and dustpan to clean up. I hadn't dropped the glass on purpose, but it felt like fate was on my side. If I hurried, I'd have at least a minute or two to look for the burner phone. If I could find it now, I could get out of here.

I couldn't count on a quick exit, though, and depending on how long I'd be recording for, I could run out of space on my phone. I couldn't be turning it on and off or Peter would notice, but if I ran out of storage before I could capture the location of the burner phone, finding it would be worthless.

My best option was to upload the video directly to my dad's online case-storage system and grab it back later. What was the mnemonic I made up for Carrie's password? Something about elephants. Three purple elephants ate rhubarb pie before bed.

I typed it in and set my phone to record video.

So, if I had just murdered my wife, and I needed to stash the evidence, what would have been easy, yet secure?

I moved alongside the pool and stuttered to a stop where the crime scene photos showed Eva Walsh's body. The closest thing to me was the planter I'd fixed the first time I came to the house. I'd even swept dirt from the planter off the path.

It couldn't be that obvious, could it? I sidled closer, trying to look casual and capture what I wanted on video without making it look like I was recording anything.

The more I thought about it, it wasn't obvious. It was brilliant. I'd assumed, as the police probably had, that the planter had been disturbed by either Eva's fall or the first responders. They'd have photographed it, but they wouldn't have dug into the dirt, thinking they might find a burner phone there—a burner phone they didn't even know they should be looking for yet. That made it a perfect spot to bury the phone.

Peter would be back any second, so I wouldn't have time to dig around in the dirt right now—dirty hands would immediately give away what I'd been doing—but I could at least take a slightly closer look. Would the plants have had time to reestablish their roots in the weeks since Eva's death, or would they still be loose?

I leaned closer and wiggled the stem of one of the geraniums.

"What are you doing?" Peter asked from behind me.

I clenched my hand around my phone. His voice was calm, but there was an underlying note that I hadn't heard before. It felt like my heart was clawing its way up into my throat, blocking my wind passage. This had been a stupid thing to do. I shouldn't be here.

Peter killed Eva for money. He'd proved he was willing to kill if he thought it would benefit him. What had made me think I'd be safe and he wouldn't hurt me? Just because he seemed to care about me? Eva probably wouldn't have stayed married to him for so many years if he hadn't seemed to care about her, too.

I had to get out of here.

"What are you doing?" Peter asked again in that too-casual tone.

I pasted a smile on my face and prayed it looked genuine. I clearly wasn't as good an actor as he was. I turned to face him. "I love this planter. I've been thinking of setting up a couple planters on the balcony of my apartment."

He took a single step closer as if he wanted to examine the planter with me. "With fall coming on?"

Crap, crap, and double crap. He knew. "For spring. But you know how I like to plan ahead." I ran a hand over the back of my neck. It came away clammy. He knew, but maybe he wasn't willing to risk a second murder, especially since he'd obviously planned Eva's carefully and mine would be spur-of-the-moment. "I'm not feeling great even after having some snacks. I think it might be better if I headed home and we took a raincheck."

I moved to step past him, but he grabbed my upper arm. "This is why you were never going to be able to hack it as a defense attorney, Nicole. As soon as you know a client is guilty, it's written all over your face."

"I don't know what you mean." I tried to pull away, but he tightened his grip to the intensity of a blood pressure cuff. "Let go of my arm."

He led me back into the house and closed the door behind us. The weight in my chest lightened. Maybe he was going to let me go after all.

He stopped in the middle of the living room. "You were supposed to be trying to defend me."

Should I drop the act or not? Curses on Peter for being so unreadable. "I have been. I thought my dad told you about how I looked in to the old client, and when I talked to Dana she even has..."

I was about to tell him Dana also had a potential motive, but his lips had narrowed into a hard line. The reason hit me too late to correct my mistake. If I'd only been looking for a way to build his defense, I wouldn't have been talking to Dana at all.

"I'm not stupid," he said. "I know what you were doing at that planter, and now I can't let you leave."

My body wanted to hyperventilate and play possum. I couldn't go there. I breathed in through my nose and let the air out my mouth. Maybe I could reason with him.

I tensed my arm against his hold in a show of resistance. "You're not stupid, which is why you're going to let me walk out of here. Think about it. Would I have come here if I could prove anything? Whatever you're thinking about doing will only create more evidence for the police to use against you."

Hopefully that would hide the fact that I'd already found evidence that poked a hole straight through his story.

He shook his head. "Doesn't matter what you can prove. If I let you leave now, I lose my insurance policy. I'm not going to prison just because you suddenly decided to grow a brain and figured out I killed Eva."

It was foolish how much that insult stung at a time when more important things were going on. Like his admission that he killed Eva, and his weird reference to me as his *insurance policy*, as if he was going to take me hostage and skip town. He was a lawyer. He knew as well as I did that taking hostages never turned out well for the hostage-taker.

My mind ground in circles as he hauled me toward the cupboard by the fridge. Whatever he had planned, it wasn't good for me. He wouldn't have admitted to murdering Eva if he planned to let me free to tell anyone.

My stomach threatened to relieve me of the cheese I'd eaten. Screaming wasn't going to help. If the neighbors couldn't hear Eva and Peter fighting, they weren't going to hear my calls for help. I could try to break away from him and make a run for the door, but I knew from the times we'd gone to the gym together that he was faster and stronger than I was.

That meant if I was getting out of here, I'd have to outthink him. I had the advantage there. I didn't know which one of us was objectively smarter, but I knew he thought he was smarter, and his underestimation of me gave me the advantage. Knowing his opinion of me meant I could manipulate it.

My phone vibrated again in my hand. I glanced down. Ahanti's name flashed across the screen, momentarily hiding the fact that the phone was still recording. He'd not only given me an advantage by underestimating my intelligence—my phone was still recording. The more I could get him to admit to on tape, the better.

Peter didn't look at the phone. He just shook his head. It didn't matter who was calling. He wasn't going to let me answer it.

"What are you planning to do?" I asked, trying to make my voice sound weak and frightened.

He poured a glass of water, set it on the counter, and pulled what looked like a multivitamin bottle from the cupboard. "I'm not going to do anything. You're going to be so overcome by guilt over the fact that you killed my wife and I'm being blamed for it, that you're going to overdose on your sleeping pills."

A shiver traced over me and my mouth dropped open. I snapped it shut again. "You took sleeping pills from my apartment?"

He popped the top with his free hand and poured a few out onto the countertop. They were identical to the ones in the prescription bottle I kept by my bed to deal with my occasional insomnia. Since I didn't take them regularly, he easily could have stored away enough for a fatal overdose without me noticing any had gone missing.

I'd once wondered if Peter could have loved both Eva and me. Now I was pretty sure the truth was he'd never loved either of us.

"How long have you been planning this?" I didn't have to fake the wobble in my voice this time.

He continued to pour pills out onto the counter. "Long enough. You're not the only one who likes to plan ahead. I knew my accident ruse might fail, which meant I needed a backup plan." The bottle ran dry and he set it aside. "Your suicide was only supposed to be a failsafe if things went badly during my trial, but now you've forced me to accelerate my plan."

I could try to guilt him into giving up on this, but if the man had no qualms about killing his wife of over ten years, he wasn't going to feel enough loyalty to my dad to spare me.

I tugged against his hold. It was like pulling again a piece of clothing caught in a closed car door. I'd tear something before I'd manage to break free. "You might be able to find a way to make me swallow those pills, but this only works the way you've planned if I write a note explaining why I killed myself. I'm not writing any note."

"If you don't, I'll write it as a text to your mom after you're out. But I'd rather spare her that."

That would destroy her. It'd be hard enough on her if she thought I'd committed suicide, but to receive my note as a text that she had to read and then call the police...she'd never be the same. If it came down to it, I'd write a lie to spare her that.

But I still had my trump card. I positioned my finger over the tiny text that said LOGOUT and held up my phone, screen facing toward Peter. The red *Recording* dot in the left-hand corner of the screen was unmistakable.

Peter cursed, and I hit LOGOUT, stopping the recording and closing down the upload program.

"How long have you been recording?" He yanked the phone from my hand. "Nevermind. I'll erase it from your phone and no one will ever see it."

"It's not stored on my phone. I uploaded it directly to Dad's case management software."

"Then I'll log in and delete it."

He typed in his email and password. I chewed the inside of my cheek. It shouldn't work. My dad had removed my access within hours. Surely he wouldn't have left Peter access to his own case.

Peter swore again.

Thank you, Dad, for being reliable.

Peter grabbed my hair and yanked my head back. "Log back in."

Yeah, because that was going to happen. I would have shaken my head, but he held me too tight to move much without pain.

He must have guessed from my expression that I wasn't going to comply. He stroked a knuckle down my exposed neck, the gesture distinctly threatening rather than tender.

"That file won't save you," he said. "Since you've screwed me, I'm going to kill you anyway. I'll be out of the country before anyone finds that file or your body."

I forced a swallow through my extended throat. He was right. Everyone had gone home for the night, possibly even for the weekend. Ahanti or Uncle Stan would worry if they couldn't reach me within a day, and Uncle Stan might guess where I'd gone, but by the time they could convince anyone to search Peter's home, he'd be long gone. He'd get away with Eva's murder and mine. Wherever he planned to go, it was likely a non-extradition country, and I had no doubt he'd been careful and methodical in stealing from Eva as Dana feared. He'd proven he'd thought of every contingency, including preparing to kill me and frame it as a suicide to ensure his freedom.

I had one chance. It was a long shot and depended on what I believed to be true about my dad and his attention to the security of our files. Peter had made a failed login to his case files. If I did the same, and he had set up an alert or tracker on my password, there was a chance he'd check the case files to make sure I hadn't found a way to get in and download anything.

If he did that, he'd see the new upload, and then it was a guarantee that he'd watch the video I'd uploaded, especially when he saw it'd been uploaded by "Carrie" rather than by a lawyer assigned to Peter's case. It might not be in time to save me, but it was the best chance I had of keeping Peter from escaping.

"If I log in for you, so you can delete the file, will you let me go?" Getting the words out was harder than I thought it would be with my stretched neck. Hopefully that would work in my favor. Peter had to believe I was desperate and gullible. "Please. I don't want to die. I promise I won't tell anyone what happened."

"Of course." Peter released my hair, and he smiled the kind of smile I would have been deceived by before. "You know I didn't want to hurt you."

Liar. He must really think I was pliable.

I forced my face to relax and took my phone back. I faked a shake in my hand, so the first failed log in would seem natural. Instead of my password, I typed in HELPMEDAD. The security he had installed on the files showed every failed log in attempt. It was a quick way to see whether someone had simply made a typo in their password or whether an unauthorized person was attempting to hack the system.

I typed it in again for my second attempt. After the third, the system locked my email address out.

The frown lines appeared between Peter's eyes again.

I bit my bottom lip. "I'm sorry. I forgot I'm locked out too. I used a stolen password to get in."

Peter's smirk was too amused for comfort. "Edward Dawes' own daughter broke into his system."

Virginia was still a death penalty state. Hopefully my dad would find a way to get that prize for Peter's arrogant condescension once he realized how I'd died. Not even my dad would defend a client for his own daughter's murder.

I typed in Carrie's email and HELPMEDAD as the password again.

The expression on Peter's face shifted. A bit of the arrogant twist to his lips slipped away. "What are you playing at? Show me what you're typing."

"I'm flustered," I said. "I'm having trouble remembering."

I quickly typed in HELPMEDAD for the password, tapping the login a fraction of a second before Peter snatched the phone back. He called me a name that would have made my mother slap him.

He grabbed my hair again and dragged me over to the counter. As hard as I fought him, I couldn't keep from swallowing all the pills he forced down my throat.

Finally exhaustion sucked me under like drowning in wet cement, even drawing a full breath a struggle. The last things I remember were hoping I'd managed to keep from swallowing enough to kill me and seeing my phone vibrate on the kitchen counter, in the same spot where Peter planted Eva's phone after killing her.

Chapter 13

I blinked my eyes open in a hospital room. Grogginess hung over me like I'd set my alarm too early, and my mouth tasted like I hadn't brushed my teeth in a week. But at least I wasn't dead. Whatever had happened after I passed out from the sleeping pills, Peter's plan had failed—or at least the part of it that involved killing me had.

A cool hand brushed the hair back from my face. "Welcome back," my mom's voice said.

I turned my head to look in her direction. If she'd been anyone else, I would have been able to guess how long I'd been out based on her appearance. My mom, though, looked like she always did. Her perfectly applied makeup hid any signs of sleeplessness, and her clothes looked like she'd picked them up from the dry cleaners moments ago. If I didn't have my mom's nose and my dad's eyes, I'd have sworn I was adopted.

"Am I going to be okay?" I said. Or more like I tried to say it. My throat didn't want to work, and the words came out with a dry crust on them.

"The doctors pumped your stomach. You'll feel sluggish for a day or two, but they say you won't have any lasting side effects."

Given how fuzzy my mind still felt, it was good to know I didn't have some sort of brain damage. "Did they catch him?"

"Yes, but..." My mom glanced back over her shoulder toward the doorway. "Your dad wants to talk to you about the Peter situation, so I don't want to say too much."

That didn't sound good. I wormed my arms out from under the blanket so I felt a little less like a swaddled child. "Can you at least tell me what happened after I passed out?"

My mom smiled a softer smile than I ever remembered seeing from her before. Her smiles usually had a sharp, almost carnivorous edge to them. "It's a bit complicated, but if I ever give you grief about your friend Ahanti again, remind me of this moment."

I vaguely remembered Ahanti calling my phone a couple of times while I was at Peter's. At first I hadn't answered because I didn't want to lie to her about where I was. Then I couldn't answer because of Peter. "What did Ahanti have to do with all this?"

My mom edged her chair a little closer and actually took my hand. She must have been really scared I might die if we'd progressed to physical expressions of affection.

"You talked to your uncle last night," she said.

Either she was jumping around or my mind was fuzzier than I thought. I nodded and a headache bloomed above my eyes. I pressed my free hand over the pounding.

"He suspected you were going to Peter's house to look for a piece of evidence you thought was there, and he was worried. Since he knew your dad wouldn't answer his call, he apparently called every tattoo parlor he could find in the area until he located Ahanti and told her his concerns."

I blinked back tears. There wasn't a way to express how much I loved Uncle Stan at that moment. Not only had he cared enough to risk sounding crazy, but he'd listened carefully enough to me over the past few years to remember Ahanti's name and her job.

"When Ahanti couldn't reach you, she called your dad. He told her you wouldn't have gone to Peter's because you'd been ordered to stay away from him." There was a wryness to her tone on the last part. I didn't know if it was linked to annoyance at me for disobeying or annoyance at my dad for dismissing the possibility out of hand. "I guess Ahanti knew better. She left work, checked your apartment in case you were there, and headed for Peter's. And you still refused to answer your phone."

There was definitely disapproval in her voice now.

I slowly worked my way into a sitting position. She tried to slide her hand away as I did, but I held tight. "What I did was stupid, I know. I won't be making that mistake again. What happened next?"

"Your dad received a security alert on his phone a few minutes later, telling him that someone was trying to hack our case-file system. When he checked and saw that every attempt used the password *HELPMEDAD*, he called the police." She grimaced. "You know how much your dad likes being wrong. When you talk to him later, just remember that anger can often be used to cover up fear. You're our only child."

I was pretty sure that anger could also simply be anger. I had no doubt he'd been worried for my safety, but I'd also wounded his pride and embarrassed him. And it seemed like he couldn't stop himself from feeling it any more than I could stop myself from wanting his approval.

"Ahanti saw your car in the driveway when she reached Peter's house and pounded on his door. The police think that's what stopped Peter from feeding you the rest of the pills that were scattered on the counter and saved your life. Even though they arrived a few minutes later, it might have been too late."

And without my dad's call, the police might not have gone at all. Ahanti was only working off of guesses and suspicion. Without Ahanti's call to him, he wouldn't have known where to send the police. Given what my mom had said, the time it took him to watch the video I'd uploaded and figure out where I'd gone would have been enough time for Peter to kill me.

My dad's figure filled the door. "I'd like to talk to her alone now."

My mom stood, breaking our hand clasp. "Ahanti will be back later today to visit."

My dad didn't take the chair my mom had vacated. Instead, he stood slightly behind it, his arms crossed over his chest, forcing me to look up at him even though I was sitting upright now.

"I turned your video over to the police," my dad said, "but they'll want your statement as well now that you're awake."

"I'm happy to give it, especially if it helps put Peter in prison."

My voice carried a touch more defiance than I'd intended. My hands ached, and I glanced down. I'd clenched the blanket in my fists. I let it go. Maybe my dad wasn't the only angry one.

"Peter's already in prison," my dad said in a dry tone. "He accepted a plea bargain."

My mouth hung open before I could stop it. "He did?"

"He didn't have a choice. The video you uploaded was difficult to argue with, and I told him if he didn't take the plea, I'd join the prosecution to bury him."

My heart felt like it swelled in my chest. That was probably as close as my dad would ever come to saying he loved me.

He uncrossed his arms and rested a hand on the back of the chair. "You disappointed me, Nicole."

And just like that my heart shrunk back to its normal size. I should have been used to it by now, but I wasn't. Every time the disappointment stung like the first. Worse, I'd probably have to still endure two more lectures from Ahanti and Uncle Stan. And I'd deserve them. Even if my dad had refused to act in favor of the truth, I'd been too mad at him to keep a clear head, and it almost got me killed. "I should have considered the potential risks and consequences more carefully before I acted."

"It puts a black mark on the reputation of our firm and on your career."

The firm and my career? That's what he was worried about? Heaven forbid a business that's willing to defend murderers gains a smudge on its reputation. As for me, we both knew I'd probably already reached the zenith of my career.

I opened my mouth to reply, but my dad held up his hand. "For once in your life, don't talk. Just listen."

I snapped my mouth shut and crossed my arms over my chest in an imitation of his earlier stance.

"When I ordered you to stay away from Peter, I was trying to protect you. I might not be able to give you commands as your father anymore, but I still can as your boss, and I expect you to obey them. I might not always be able to clean up your messes."

My arms slumped to my sides. He had a point there. If I worked for anyone else, I'd be fired right now. "Yes, sir."

"But few people would have thought to use my system against me that way. Make sure you use that intelligence to keep yourself *out* of dangerous situations next time."

I kept my mouth closed by a sheer act of will this time. If I didn't know better, I'd almost think that had been a compliment.

My dad turned on his heel and headed for the door. "And you'd better call your uncle."

All I could do was blink in response. It was the first time in over a decade that one of my parents suggested I contact Uncle Stan.

Maybe miracles did happen after all. And maybe that meant there was still hope for my dad and me yet.

BONUS RECIPE

Nicole's Favorite French Toast

INGREDIENTS:

2 eggs

1 cup milk (you can use any milk you like, including coconut or almond milk)

Pinch salt

1 tablespoon maple syrup

1 teaspoon vanilla extract

1/2 teaspoon cinnamon

Large French baguette

INSTRUCTIONS:

1. Whisk together everything except the bread and pour it into a flat-bottomed baking dish.

2. Cut bread into 1/2 inch slices. Place bread slices into egg mixture and flip to coat.
3. Either melt butter in a pan or spray a pan with non-stick cooking spray (depending on how healthy you want to be). Place bread slices in pan and cook until golden brown on both sides.
4. Serve with warmed maple syrup.

MAKES approximately 16 slices.

LETTER FROM THE AUTHOR

Thank you so much for coming back with me to visit Nicole before she ended up in Fair Haven. I hope you had fun learning a little bit about her history.

Because I have many more adventures in store for Nicole, Mark, Erik, and the others, I'm putting together a Pre-Release Reader Team. If you join, you'll receive an ebook copy of each book before it's available for purchase. All I ask in return is that you leave an honest review for that book. To join the team, simply send me an email at authoremilyjames@gmail.com.

If you don't want to join the team but you'd still like to know as soon as the next book releases, sign up for my newsletter at www.smarturl.it/emilyjames.

ABOUT THE AUTHOR

Emily James grew up watching TV shows like *Matlock*, *Monk*, and *Murder She Wrote*. (It's pure coincidence that they all begin with an M.) It was no surprise to anyone when she turned into a mystery writer.

She loves cats, dogs, and coffee. Lots and lots of coffee...lots and lots of cats too. Seriously, there's hardly room in the bed for her husband. While they only have one dog, she's a Great Dane, so she should count as at least two.

If you'd like to know as soon as Emily's next mystery releases, please join her newsletter list at www.smarturl.it/emilyjames.

She also loves hearing from readers. You can email her through her website (www.authoremilyjames.com) or find her on Facebook (www.facebook.com/authoremilyjames/).